He wondered when he'd last been so happily unselfconscious.... Perhaps never.

Dottie's radiant innocence was like a blow to his heart. She was so candid and trusting, so sure the rest of the world was as honest as herself.

How could she realize that the man with her was the serpent in Eden, plotting to destroy her happiness?

For he was about to turn her world upside down, starting with the very world in which she was at ease, then he would shake things up with the lover who meant so much to her. And in their place he offered wealth, grandeur and a kind of power—all of which, Randolph was increasingly convinced, would mean nothing to her. But perhaps a great love would be discovered in the meantime....

Dear Reader,

This August, I am delighted to give you six winning reasons to pick up a Silhouette Special Edition book.

For starters, Lindsay McKenna, whose action-packed and emotionally gritty romances have entertained readers for years, moves us with her exciting cross-line series MORGAN'S MERCENARIES: ULTIMATE RESCUE. The first book, *The Heart Beneath,* tells of love against unimaginable odds. With a background as a firefighter in the late 1980s, Lindsay elaborates, "This story is about love, even when buried beneath the rubble of a hotel, or deep within a human being who has been terribly wounded by others, that it will not only survive, but emerge and be victorious."

No stranger to dynamic storytelling, Laurie Paige kicks off a new MONTANA MAVERICKS spin-off with *Her Montana Man,* in which a beautiful forensics examiner must gather evidence in a murder case, but also has to face the town's mayor, a man she'd loved and lost years ago. Don't miss the second book in THE COLTON'S: COMANCHE BLOOD series—Jackie Merritt's *The Coyote's Cry,* a stunning tale of forbidden love between a Native American sheriff and the town's "golden girl."

Christine Rimmer delivers the first romance in her captivating new miniseries THE SONS OF CAITLIN BRAVO. In *His Executive Sweetheart,* a secretary pines for a Bravo bachelor who just happens to be her boss! And in Lucy Gordon's *Princess Dottie,* a waitress-turned-princess is a dashing prince's only chance at keeping his kingdom—and finding true love.… Debut author Karen Sandler warms readers with *The Boss's Baby Bargain,* in which a controlling CEO strikes a marriage bargain with his financially strapped assistant, but their smoldering attraction leads to an unexpected pregnancy!

This month's selections are stellar romances that will put a smile on your face and a song in your heart! Happy reading.

Sincerely,

Karen Taylor Richman
Senior Editor

Please address questions and book requests to:
Silhouette Reader Service
U.S.: 3010 Walden Ave., P.O. Box 1325, Buffalo, NY 14269
Canadian: P.O. Box 609, Fort Erie, Ont. L2A 5X3

Princess Dottie

LUCY GORDON

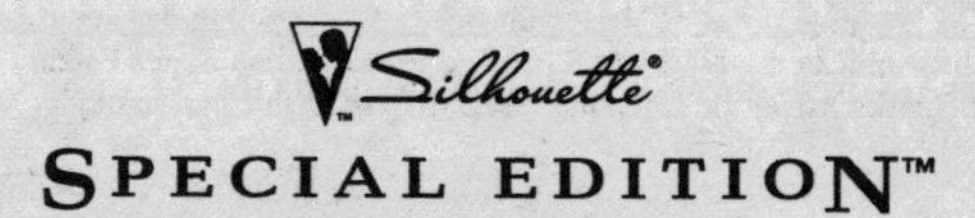

Published by Silhouette Books
America's Publisher of Contemporary Romance

If you purchased this book without a cover you should be aware that this book is stolen property. It was reported as "unsold and destroyed" to the publisher, and neither the author nor the publisher has received any payment for this "stripped book."

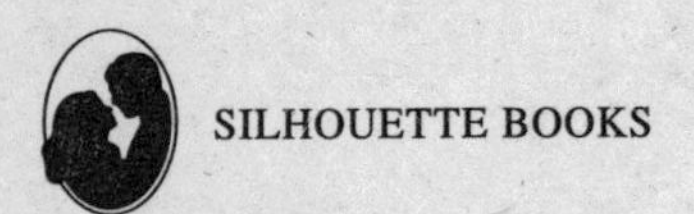

ISBN 0-373-24487-8

PRINCESS DOTTIE

Copyright © 2002 by Lucy Gordon

All rights reserved. Except for use in any review, the reproduction or utilization of this work in whole or in part in any form by any electronic, mechanical or other means, now known or hereafter invented, including xerography, photocopying and recording, or in any information storage or retrieval system, is forbidden without the written permission of the editorial office, Silhouette Books, 300 East 42nd Street, New York, NY 10017 U.S.A.

All characters in this book have no existence outside the imagination of the author and have no relation whatsoever to anyone bearing the same name or names. They are not even distantly inspired by any individual known or unknown to the author, and all incidents are pure invention.

This edition published by arrangement with Harlequin Books S.A.

® and TM are trademarks of Harlequin Books S.A., used under license. Trademarks indicated with ® are registered in the United States Patent and Trademark Office, the Canadian Trade Marks Office and in other countries.

Visit Silhouette at www.eHarlequin.com

Printed in U.S.A.

Books by Lucy Gordon

Silhouette Special Edition

Legacy of Fire #148
Enchantment in Venice #185
Bought Woman #547
Outcast Woman #749
Seduced by Innocence #902
Forgotten Fiancée #1112
Anything, Any Time, Any Place #1227
For His Little Girl #1348
Princess Dottie #1487

Silhouette Romance

The Carrister Pride #306
Island of Dreams #353
Virtue and Vice #390
Once Upon a Time #420
A Pearl Beyond Price #503
Golden Boy #524
A Night of Passion #596
A Woman of Spirit #611
A True Marriage #639
Song of the Lorelei #754
Heaven and Earth #904
Instant Father #952
This Man and This Woman #1079

Silhouette Desire

Take All Myself #164
The Judgement of Paris #179
A Coldhearted Man #245
My Only Love, My Only Hate #317
A Fragile Beauty #333
Just Good Friends #363
Eagle's Prey #380
For Love Alone #416
Vengeance Is Mine #493
Convicted of Love #544
The Sicilian #627
On His Honor #669
Married in Haste #777
Uncaged #864
Two Faced Woman #953
This Is My Child #982
Blood Brothers #1307
"Randall"

LUCY GORDON

met her husband-to-be in Venice, fell in love the first evening and got engaged two days later. They're still happily married and now live in England with their three dogs. For twelve years, Lucy was a writer for an English women's magazine. She interviewed many of the world's most interesting men, including Warren Beatty, Richard Chamberlain, Sir Roger Moore, Sir Alec Guinness and Sir John Gielgud.

In 1985 she won the *Romantic Times* Reviewers' Choice Award for Outstanding Series Romance Author. She has also won a Golden Leaf Award from the New Jersey Chapter of RWA, was a finalist in the RWA Golden Medallion contest in 1988 and won the 1990 RITA® Award in the Best Traditional Romance category for *Song of the Lorelei*.

THE ANCIENT AND ROYAL HOUSE OF ALLINBURG

Queen Dorothea I m. Friedrich of Korburg

King Randolph II m. Queen Sophia

King Hector m. Antonia

Queen Dorothea II

King Randolph III

King Randolph IV

King Egbert I

Prince Randolph

Duke Egbert m. Sonia

Dorothea m. Augustus Hebden

Randolph Hebden

Jack Hebden

Frank Hebden

Dorothea ("Dottie") Hebden

Dorothea

Duke Alphonse m. Elsa

Leon

Lionel

Sarah m. Prince Joseph of Korburg

Prince Harold of Korburg

Prologue

The hands of the clock crawled toward nine o'clock. Another long shift over, Dottie thought thankfully. Fifteen more minutes and she'd be out of the café. Until tomorrow, when it would be time to start again.

Her face brightened as the door opened and a beefy young man with an amiable expression, came in, waved to her and slid into a corner seat. She mouthed, "With you in a minute."

A plump, dark-haired young woman appeared from the kitchen and made a beeline for the lad, Dottie noted wryly. She knew Brenda fancied Mike, and wasn't ashamed to make a play for him right under Dottie's nose, although she knew they were engaged.

Despite its name, The Grand Hotel was a down-at-heel boardinghouse with a café to match, in the shabbiest part of London. Dottie ran the café, and Jack, the elderly owner, had bestowed on her the title of manageress to cover the fact that she was a maid-of-all-work, who slaved long, tiring hours for a small wage.

Yet Dottie was happy. She had a fiancé she loved and a future to look forward to. Mike might not be glamorous, but he was kind, hardworking and devoted to her. True, his brain lacked the quicksilver alertness of her own. Unkind persons had been known to describe him as thick. Dottie would have been up in arms at that slander, but when her own mind went dancing away she sometimes wished he could follow her, instead of just saying admiringly, "You sound grand when you talk like that, Dot."

Mike was proud of his fiancée: proud of her petite figure and fluffy blond prettiness, proud of her quick tongue, her shrewdness and her ability to laugh at herself. But he never pretended he could keep up with her.

As Dottie cleared away, Jack appeared and began to cash up. "Has it been a good evening, Dorothea?" he asked kindly.

Dottie made a face. "I wish you wouldn't call me Dorothea."

The old man grinned. "Perhaps I should call you Ms. Hebden, then?"

"You do and you're dead," she told him amiably. "Dottie's good enough for me."

"There's a few hamburgers left over," Jack said. "If you fancy them."

She scooped them up eagerly. This was a valuable perk for people who were living on nothing so that Mike could save up for his own garage. She bid Jack good-night and headed for the corner table, tapping Brenda firmly on the shoulder.

"Hands off! He's mine!" But she said it with a good-natured smile.

Brenda grinned back. "Bet he's not. Bet I could have him off you."

"Bet you couldn't!"

"Bet I could!"

"Oi!" Mike objected mildly. "D'you two mind not talking about me like I wasn't here?"

He allowed his fiancée to shepherd him to the door, only pausing to call back, "Better check your food for arsenic tomorrow, Bren."

"Well if I do poison her it'll be your fault," Dottie said when they were outside. "Serve her right for putting her head so close to yours."

"It was just gossip," Mike protested. "She's been reading that magazine again. *Royal Secrets.*"

"Her and her royal scandals! That's all she thinks of. What is it this time?"

"The king of Elluria can't be the king 'cos his parents weren't properly wed."

Dottie yawned. "Well, they'll find another one. Come on, I've got some free hamburgers."

"Good for you! I'm starving."

Chapter One

The avenue of lime trees stretched into the distance, the tips faintly touched by the crimson of the setting sun. Randolph regarded with indifference a scene he'd watched a thousand times before. It was as useful as listening to the conversation going on behind him, which he'd also been through a thousand times before—or at least it felt like it. And while he kept his back to the room nobody could study his face.

He was wearily used to that study. Ever since he'd been barred from the throne of Elluria barely hours before assuming it, the world was curious about his feelings. Sometimes he felt like a caged animal, staring back at faces pressed against the bars, all watching him for some sign of weakness. And he would die before he revealed such a sign.

These days his expression was habitually grim. He was a serious man who normally found little in life to make him laugh, although he secretly envied those who could. Recently heaviness had overcome him completely. Those who might have been his subjects had known what to expect from him, gravity and devotion to duty, tempered with a quiet, stern kindliness. Now they were almost afraid of him.

The prime minister, Jacob Durmand, approached him nervously. "Your Royal…Your Highness…oh dear!" He lapsed into confusion at having used the term "royal" to one who could no longer be described that way.

Randolph turned, forcing a brief, reassuring smile. It wasn't Durmand's fault. "It's a trial to all of us," he said. "Don't worry about it."

"Thank you. Oh dear, this is all very difficult. If only—"

"If only my dear, scatterbrained father hadn't fallen in love with an actress when he was young," Randolph said wryly, "and been persuaded to go through a marriage ceremony when he was too drunk to know better. If only he hadn't believed those who said it wasn't binding. And if only he'd made sure of his situation before marrying my mother. But you knew my father, Durmand. He was the kindest man in the world, but he had this fatal habit of hoping for the best."

"And if only Prince Harold hadn't discovered that your parents' marriage was bigamous," the prime minister sighed. "Once he knew, he was bound to pounce, hoping to take the throne himself."

"And get his hands on Elluria's mineral reserves," Randolph said angrily. "How long would it take him to strip the country of everything? He's got to be stopped. Dammit, this family must have some offshoots left somewhere in the world.''

He was interrupted by an elderly man scurrying into the room, his arms full of papers, his face full of excitement. He was Sigmund, the royal archivist.

''I've found something,'' he said.

They all crowded around the table while he spread the papers out.

''It goes back to Duke Egbert, who married an English lady in 1890,'' he explained. ''She was an heiress, and he had heavy gambling debts. They went to live in England.''

''Are you saying there are descendants there?'' Durmand asked.

''One, as far as I can gather. And I'm afraid the family has come down in the world—gambling again. The duke had one daughter who married a man called Augustus Hebden. It's his great-great-great-granddaughter who concerns us. It's been carefully checked. The line is unbroken.''

''Did Egbert really leave no other descendants?'' Randolph asked.

''The family was almost wiped out in two wars,'' Sigmund explained. ''In the end there was only Jack Hebden left, plus his sister, who never married. Jack had one child, Frank, who fathered the lady with whom we are concerned. Ms. Dorothea Hebden is next in line to the throne of Elluria.''

''Do we know anything else?'' Durmand inquired nervously. ''Has she encumbered herself with a husband and a brood of children?''

''Fortunately no,'' Sigmund said, too deep in papers to notice that Randolph had stiffened. ''Exhaustive inquiries have failed to turn up a marriage certificate. She is only twenty-three, but has already risen to the position of manageress of an establishment called The Grand Hotel."

"This looks encouraging," Durmand said. "This young woman must be talented, hardworking and educated with an orderly mind."

"That doesn't mean she'll want to come to Elluria," Randolph pointed out.

"To have risen so high, so young she must also be ambitious," Durmand said hastily. "She will welcome the chance to broaden her horizons."

"My dear Prime Minister, you're creating a fantasy figure to suit yourself," Randolph said sharply. "You have only to add that a hotel manageress's training is the ideal basis to become queen of Elluria."

"In so far as it requires elegance and authority, that may be true," Durmand defended himself.

Randolph sighed. "Perhaps I can't blame you. We're all hoping for the best. Let us hope that she is the paragon of your imagination."

"There's only one way to find out," Durmand said. "She must be sought out and brought here without delay."

When he left the room Randolph headed for the elegant apartment that was reserved for Countess Sophie Bekendorf when she was visiting the palace. She'd been there often recently, preparing for the wedding that would make her Randolph's princess, and eventually his queen. Her life too had been overturned, he reminded himself. She was five years his junior, and their marriage had been planned in her cradle. He admired her and knew how perfectly she would have adorned a throne.

She smiled and rose when he entered, crossing the floor quickly, looking into his face. Her tall slim figure had been tautened by hours of riding. Her face was beautiful, though marred by a slight hardness in her eyes. Her manners were elegant and commanding. She knew who was worthy of her smiles, and who not.

She was all anxiety, taking Randolph's hand. "Was it very bad, my poor dear?" she asked gently.

"Worse than I can say. The heir turns out to be a hotel manageress in England. Her name is Dorothea Hebden."

"It's impossible!" she said violently. "A servant."

"Not quite. She seems to have achieved some authority—"

"Tradesman's authority. A servant."

"I suppose we mustn't judge without seeing her. We might be able to make something of her."

"You don't mean you're considering this monstrous idea for one moment?"

He led her back to the window and looked out over the great park. This way it was easier to voice his thoughts.

"It's not a matter of what I will agree to. My authority ended the moment we discovered that I was illegitimate. Now I'm not even royal. Dorothea Hebden is the rightful heir to the throne of Elluria."

"Have you thought she might be married?"

"Sigmund seems sure that she isn't."

"I see," Sophie said quietly.

Something in her tone made him put his arms around her. "I left soon after that because I could see the way Durmand's mind was working, and I didn't like it. My dear, how can I forget that when I offered to release you from our engagement, you refused, and stood by me so steadfastly?''

''You thought I'd turn my back on you because you had no crown to offer?''

''If I did, I was wrong,'' he said tenderly. ''No man could ask for more courage and loyalty that you've shown me—''

''But you may have to marry this other woman,'' she interrupted him. ''Perhaps it will be you who breaks our engagement, for duty. I understand, and you are free. But if it doesn't come to that—'' she broke off, her voice husky.

Randolph was confused and embarrassed. From the country's point of view the ideal solution was for him to marry Princess Dorothea, ''this interloper'' as he thought of her. Then, under the guise of being her consort, he would rule Elluria as he had been raised to do, and nobody would care about his feelings for Sophie, or hers for him.

He'd never pretended to be in love with her, but they were friends, and he was furious at being required to behave badly toward her. It offended his sense of himself, and there was much haughty pride in it. But there was also much generosity. The situation was very bitter to him, and not merely on his own account.

He wasn't a conceited man, but now it seemed to him that Sophie had more true feeling for him than he'd suspected, and that touched his conscience. Perhaps she knew this, and was pleased. She was a very clever woman.

Sophie's brother Dagbert sauntered in. He was in his early twenties, strikingly like his sister, except that too much self-indulgence was already beginning to show in his face.

''So what are you going to do?'' he demanded when Randolph had outlined the situation. ''Pity it's not a century ago. We could have had her assassinated.''

''That wouldn't make me legitimate,'' Randolph pointed out. ''I intend to bring her here, and see how we can make the best of it.''

''You mean you'll marry her and carry on as before,'' Dagbert said sharply.

''He means that we shall all do our duty,'' Sophie said. ''Whatever it may be.''

Randolph pressed her hand in gratitude, and made his escape. He found Dagbert's callow vulgarity oppressive.

When brother and sister were alone the young man regarded her through narrowed eyes. ''What deep game are you playing, Soph?''

''I don't know what you mean.''

''Yes you do. Why cling to the engagement? You ought to be hunting bigger game.''

''What makes you think I'm not?''

Dagbert gave a crack of laughter. ''I see. Keep him on the string just in case.''

''What have I got to lose? This English servant won't come to anything. Randolph is still the biggest 'game' in Europe.''

''Except for Harold.''

''Harold's marrying that woman with the millionaire father.''

''That's been put on hold,'' Dagbert murmured. ''Harold thinks his prospects are improving every day. But you're right. Keep your options open—just in case."

Randolph's trip to England was made incognito. His secretary made a reservation at The Grand Hotel in the name of Edmond Holsson, and a special passport in that name was hurriedly produced by the Ellurian Ministry of the Interior. Thus armed, Randolph flew to London, and took a taxi straight to the hotel.

He had often visited friends in England, but they lived in the great country houses that were like palaces, or in Mayfair, the most expensive part of London. He'd never ventured to the shabbier parts of the city, and didn't even know where they were. So the hotel's address, in an area of London called Wenford, set off no alarm bells in his head. But as the cab took him farther away from the city center and his surroundings grew poorer and more dreary the alarm bells began ringing with a vengeance. When the driver sang out, "Here it is!" he stepped out and regarded the place with horror.

The Grand Hotel was a narrow, three-floor building of peeling paintwork and red brick that needed repair. It was evening and the pink neon sign was on. Some of the letters were missing, so that the sign actually read The Gran Hot.

Inside was a poorly lit hall and a reception desk, but no receptionist. Randolph rang the bell and an elderly man in shirtsleeves emerged from some inner region.

"Good evening," Randolph said politely. "I have a reservation. Edmond Holsson."

"Right," Jack said, eyeing the stranger's expensive clothes and air of breeding. "If you'll just sign here, sir, you're in Number 7. It's all ready—that is—'' a thought seemed to strike him and he added quickly, ''would you be wanting something to eat? The hotel restaurant closes in half an hour. It's an excellent place. My manageress takes personal charge of it.''

''Would that be Ms. Dorothea Hebden?'' Randolph asked cautiously.

''It would indeed, sir. Have you heard of her?''

''Of the excellence of her work,'' Randolph confirmed.

''Well, just go through that door over there. The porter will take your bags up.''

With deep foreboding Randolph passed through the connecting door and found himself in a café whose chief merit was its cheerfulness. The tabletops were laminate, in a truly vile shade of red. Worse still was a small palm tree made of plastic that was clearly meant to dress up its surroundings. Randolph gazed at the palm, dumbstruck at its sheer awfulness.

The waitress, a dainty blonde with fluffy hair and the face of a mischievous imp, called out to him, ''Sit down, love. I'll be over in a minute.''

Randolph didn't want to sit down in this place but his knees were threatening to give way with shock, so he found a corner table that was partly concealed by the palm, and tried to be inconspicuous. It was hard because, surrounded by men in shirtsleeves and overalls, he was the only one in a proper suit.

Where was the high-class establishment of his imagining? A mirage. Instead, this. *This!* And he'd committed himself to spending the night in the place. He'd told himself that no sacrifice was too great for his country. Now he began to wonder if he'd been wrong.

The waitress was gathering plates vigorously. At the table behind her a young man leaned across and patted her behind, making her turn with a little squeal and a reproving, "Hey, watch it!"

"Sorry," the young man said, grinning. "Couldn't help myself."

"Looks to me like you *were* helping yourself," she riposted. "Keep your hands off or I'll set Mike on you." She was laughing as she eased away from him, wriggling gracefully to avoid his hand again.

A good-natured young woman, Randolph thought, but hardly the person he sought.

Another waitress bustled out from the kitchen. She was dark, comely and extremely well built. She called out, "Dottie, do you want me to do the corner table?"

"No thanks Bren, I've grabbed him," the blonde sang back. She waved at Randolph and called cheerily, "You don't mind me grabbing you, do you love?"

"Not at all," he replied politely, trying to conceal his growing dismay. Dottie! Dorothea? *This was Princess Dorothea?*

At that moment one of the men at the table whispered something to her and she went into peals of laughter. It was a delightful sound, rich and resonant, full of the joy of life. But princesses did not laugh in that unrestrained way.

She scurried over to Randolph, and sat down at the chair opposite with a sigh of relief. "Okay if I sit down to take your order? It's been a long day and my feet are killing me."

A flash of inspiration came to Randolph. He assumed an air of hauteur to say, "As a matter of fact, it's not 'Okay.'"

She rose at once. "All right, all right, keep your hair on."

"Keep—my—hair—on?" he echoed in bewilderment, feeling the top of his head. "Are you impertinent enough to suggest that I'm wearing a wig?"

Again her laughter bubbled up. "Blimey no! It's just an expression. It means don't get worked up. Keep your hair on."

"But why hair?"

"I don't know. It's just, well, you're not English, are you?"

"Is that a crime?" he asked sternly.

"No, it's just that it's an English expression and, well, you're not English, so you don't understand it." She made a wry face. "I think I've said enough."

"More than enough," he said coldly. "Now, if you don't mind, I should like something to eat."

"Sausage and beans? Sausage and fries? Sausage and bacon? Sausage and eggs?"

"Do you do anything that doesn't come with sausage?"

"Hamburger with beans? Hamburger with fries, ham—"

"Thank you, I get the picture," he said hastily. "You'll pardon me for saying that the cuisine hardly lives up to the place's name."

"Cuisine? Oh, posh food. No love, nothing posh about us."

"So I gather," he murmured heavily.

"Pardon?"

"Nothing. Down here it says 'liver and bacon'—"

"Sorry, liver's off. It's the end of the day. We ran out an hour ago."

"Rabbit stew?"

"We ran out of that two hours ago." She checked her watch. "And you'll have to be quick. We close soon."

"Close? With an unsatisfied customer?"

"Well, if we could find something you like—"

"But I've already found two things that I like, and you said they're both off," he said, trying to sound peevish. He was really getting into the skin of the part now, seeking the point where her patience would fray. Turning the screw a little further, he added acidly, "This hardly seems a very well-run establishment."

"It's a little backstreet café, not the flamin' Ritz," she protested. "I know what my customers like and I cater for it."

"You're not doing so well with me."

"But you're not like the others. You *should* be at the Ritz. Are you sure you came to the right place?"

"Unfortunately, yes," he responded in a hollow voice.

"So what'll it be?"

"Since it all looks equally disgusting," he snapped, "you'd better bring me anything that isn't 'off.' That is, if you can find something."

That should test her temper to the limit, he thought. But when he looked up she was regarding him with quizzical amusement.

"You've had a hard day too, haven't you?" she asked kindly.

"Yes," he said, suddenly dazed. "Yes—"

"What's the matter?"

"I—nothing."

"Why are you staring at me like that?"

"I'm not. Just bring me the first dish you lay your hands on."

He was glad when she left. He needed a moment to come to terms with his sudden sense of shock. It was nothing that could be precisely defined, just a strange sensation when he'd surprised that odd kindness on her face.

Suddenly he was a child again, with his Aunt Gertrude, his father's sister who'd raised him after his mother died. The boy had been throwing a temper about some childish tragedy. And when he'd kicked the furniture and shouted unforgivable things in his frustration and misery he'd looked up, expecting anger, but encountered instead his aunt's understanding smile.

"Why don't we just forget all about it?" she asked tenderly. And he'd known that she was the kindest person in the world. As well as the prettiest.

He could see Aunt Gertrude now, her pixie face with its halo of soft blond hair, so like the waitress's. There could be no doubt about it. Impossible as it seemed, this was a member of the Ellurian royal dynasty, bearing the family face down through the generations.

His rudeness hadn't fazed her, and he had to give her high marks for her patience and self-control. But oh, her voice! Her laugh! Her way of calling him "love"! And this woman was the rightful monarch of Elluria! He could have wept for his country.

She returned with a plate of pie and peas.

"Sit down," he said, indicating the seat opposite. She gave him a wary look and he nodded. "I'm not consistent, am I? But I'm a stranger here and I'd like to talk."

"All right," she sat down with a sigh of relief.

"It must be a hard job," he said sympathetically.

She groaned. "Tell me about it!" Then she laughed. "But I enjoy it. You meet people."

"Do you live on the premises? I understand you're the manageress."

She giggled. "Manageress! Honestly! That's just one of Jack's harmless daydreams, like calling this place The Grand. I mean, look at it. He's a sweet old boy, but you've got to admit it's hilarious."

Randolph, who was feeling anything but amused, agreed that it was.

"So you don't live here?" he continued valiantly.

"I've got a room a few streets away."

"You're not married?" Randolph asked cautiously. He no longer dared rely on any of Sigmund's information.

"Not yet, but Mike and I will be setting the day soon. That's him, over there."

Randolph followed her gaze to the stocky young man who was just coming through the door. From his stained overalls he seemed to be a mechanic. He waved at Dottie, then settled down in a corner table.

"No other family?" Randolph persisted. "Father? Mother?"

"My parents died years ago."

"Brothers or sisters?"

"No."

"Ex-husbands?"

"No. Excuse me," she said with sudden determination, "I've got some urgent business to attend to."

She jumped up, hurried over to the young man, just getting there ahead of the dark-haired waitress, and planted a firm kiss on his mouth. "Push off," she told Brenda. "Find your own feller."

"You can talk." Brenda addressed herself to Mike. "She's been all over that bloke behind the palm. Can't see his face but his clothes are posh."

"Eee, Dot," Mike said, awed, "have you got a rich admirer?"

"Could be," Dottie agreed.

"He's been asking her all sorts of personal stuff," Brenda went on. "Like, has she got any family?"

"What's he want to do that for?" Mike asked, puzzled.

"White slavery," Brenda said dramatically.

Dottie stared. "You *what?*"

"He's the front man, luring innocent girls into his net, then selling them on," Brenda said with relish. "He's probably stocking a harem. He's asking all those questions because he wants to know if anyone will be looking for you."

"Then why isn't he asking you questions?" Dottie wanted to know.

"There's a better market in blondes. He's probably got your purchaser already lined up."

Mike was impressed. "Hey, Dot, do you think he'd give me two camels for you?"

"You cheeky blighter!" she said indignantly. "What do you mean, two? Three, or you're dead."

"Well, tell him I'm open to offers. Three camels would just about pay the deposit on that garage."

This sent Dottie into gales of laughter. Still shaking, she made her way unsteadily back to Randolph's table, and collapsed into her seat.

"What's so funny?" Randolph demanded, fascinated. He'd only caught odd scraps of the conversation.

It took her some time to get the words out between chuckles, but when she'd finished he gave a reluctant grin. Despite his gloomy mood he found her sunny approach to life infectious.

"I'm afraid I'm not anything as interesting as a white slaver," he said.

"Pity," Dottie said, making a face. "I could sell you Brenda at a discount. That would make her leave my fiancé alone."

"She's certainly making eyes at him. And he doesn't seem to mind."

"Oh, Mike's an innocent," Dottie said cheerfully. "He needs me to look after him."

"Shouldn't he be looking after you?"

"We look after each other, we always have, ever since we were at school. On my first day, someone knocked me down in the playground and he picked me up and stopped them doing it again. And I helped him with his sums."

Yes, Randolph thought uncharitably, the bumpkin looked like someone who would need help with his sums.

"Is that all you want out of life," he asked, "to settle down with a garage mechanic?"

"What's wrong with him being a garage mechanic?" she fired up.

"Nothing," he said hastily, reading dire retribution in her eyes. "I just thought you might have been a bit more ambitious."

"Why?" she asked, honestly baffled.

"Because a girl as pretty as you could take her pick of men."

"Do you really think I'm pretty?"

"Ravishing," he said, adding shamelessly, "With that tiny waist and those smoky blue eyes, you could be a model."

"You *are* a white slaver," she said triumphantly. "I must tell Mike. He said you could have me for three camels."

Randolph felt all at sea. Nothing in his previous life had prepared him for a woman who turned everything into a joke.

"Why does he want three camels?" he asked, grasping at straws.

"When he's sold them he can afford the deposit on a garage."

"I'm not sure how much three camels would fetch," he mused, keeping gamely up with her.

"Well if it's not enough we'll throw Brenda in as well, for another two."

"Only two?"

"Well, she's not worth as many as me," Dottie said with such indignation that he laughed. "He's not just a mechanic," she added. "He's going to be an owner."

"And who'll do the sums?" Randolph asked, touched by her eagerness.

"Me of course. Mike's genius is in his hands."

"And did you, by any chance, put the idea into his head?"

"I may have done."

"And who found the garage?"

"Well, me."

"And who's been talking with the bank? Mike?"

Dottie crowed with laughter and thumped him on the shoulder in a familiar way that nobody had ever dared do before. For an instant he stiffened, but then he remembered he was incognito and forced himself to relax.

"It's no use you trying to make me think Mike is thick."

"I can see that," he murmured wryly.

"Anyway, I don't care. He's mine."

The sudden softening of her voice, and a glow in her eyes made Randolph ask quietly, "You really love him, don't you?"

"Heaps and heaps," Dottie said with a happy sigh.

"So you wouldn't be interested in my nefarious intentions?"

"Nef— What?"

"It means 'up to no good.' That's what you think of me?"

"I've got to, while you're in that posh gear," she said cheekily. "The last bloke who came in here dressed like that was arrested as he went out the door. Got five years for fraud."

"Then since my clothes have given me away, you'd better tell me something about yourself so that I can decide whether you're worth three camels."

That made her crow with laughter, and to his ears it had a pleasant sound.

"My name's Dottie Hebden," she said, unwittingly sinking his last hope. "It's short for Dorothea. I ask you! Fancy saddling someone with a name like Dorothea!"

"Perhaps it's a family name."

"Funny you should say that because as a matter of fact it is. According to my grandpa, anyway. If you believed him we come from a grand family, years and years ago."

"Did he ever tell you anything about this family?"

"I'm not sure. The trouble was, he was a terrible man for the drink, and when he was tipsy everyone stopped listening. No, it was just Grandpa spinning pretty tales."

"Haven't you ever wished that they were true?"

"Heavens no! What, me? Swanning about in a tiara and acting grand? Don't be funny!"

Her smile died as something attracted her attention. Randolph followed her gaze and saw that Mike was talking into a mobile phone, looking as annoyed as his good-natured face would allow. He finished the call, shrugged helplessly at Dottie and rose to his feet.

"Sorry, love," he said, coming across. "Gotta go out and see to a breakdown. Important customer. It sounds like a long job, so I won't see you tonight. Never mind. Tomorrow's half day. Meet you in the park as usual."

He kissed her cheek and departed.

"Oh heck!" Dottie sighed. "Just when we're about to close. Brenda, come and help me clear up. Brenda? *Brenda?*"

"I'm afraid she's gone," Randolph told her. "She slipped out straight after Mike."

"The lousy, rotten... She's not supposed to leave until I say so. You wouldn't believe it, but I'm supposed to be the manageress here." Dottie stood in the middle of the floor, raised her fluffy head to heaven and cried, "I am Authority, with a capital *A*. Underlings tremble when I talk to them." There was a cheer from the other customers, evidently used to this, and she reverted to normal. "But for all the notice she takes of me I might as well be the dogsbody. In fact,

I *am* the dogsbody, because now I've got to clear up on my own."

"I'm afraid that's the price of scaling managerial heights," Randolph said sympathetically.

Dottie pointed a sausage at him. "*You* can hush!"

She went around the tables collecting money, and the café slowly emptied. As she started the washing up a wall phone buzzed. Under cover of taking his crockery to the counter Randolph shamelessly eavesdropped, but it gained him little. Dottie's face, full of exasperation, was more revealing.

"I'll strangle Jack," she said, hanging up. "Someone called Holsson made a reservation for tonight and Jack forgot to tell me, so I've got to get his room ready before I go. Oh blast Jack. I hope his milk curdles and his socks rot. And the same goes for Mr. Holsson, whoever he is."

Chapter Two

"I'm afraid you have to go now," Dottie said. "I'm locking up."

"Can't I help you clear away to atone for my crime?"

"Crime?"

"I'm the awkward Mr. Holsson," he confessed.

"Oh heck!" She clasped her hand over her mouth, looking so much like a guilty child that he had to laugh. "Me and my big gob! I'm always doing it."

"Don't worry. I won't tell anyone if you don't."

"I'm not usually this disorganized."

"It's not your fault if nobody told you."

"Thanks. That's nice of you. Just give me a minute and I'll be over there to make you comfortable."

Randolph felt that nothing short of a miracle could make him comfortable in this nightmarish place, but he held his tongue. He was growing to like Dottie.

She was loudmouthed, over-the-top and totally unsuitable to be a queen, but she had a rough good nature that appealed to him, and her ability to laugh in the face of her dreary life touched his heart.

She was just finishing the cashing up. "This is supposed to be Jack's job," she sighed.

"But tonight he's giving you a wide berth," Randolph reminded her. "That way you can't complain about his 'high crimes and misdemeanors'."

"His whaters?" Dottie asked, her eyes on the till.

"His failure to pass on the message."

"Oh, I see. Why not say so in English?"

"It *is* English," Randolph said, suppressing a desire to tear his hair.

"Not where I come from."

He drew a long breath. It was her language, wasn't it? If he could speak it, why couldn't she?

But he abandoned the subject as fruitless. "Since this is partly my fault, why don't you let me help you clear up?" he suggested.

She agreed to this readily, and within a few minutes they had finished. She vanished into a little room at the rear to remove her waitress uniform, and returned in a blouse that looked faded from much washing, and shorts that revealed a pair of dazzling legs.

He had a sudden aching memory of his much loved but erratic father, a "leg man" and proud of it. Gazing at Dottie's shining pins Randolph wondered if he had more in common with his wayward parent than he'd suspected.

She locked up, turned out the lights and together they went next door, where, despite Jack's promise about a porter, Randolph's bags were still standing in the hall where he'd left them. It was a measure of how far he'd traveled in the past hour that this didn't surprise him.

Room 7 came as a nasty shock. With his first step he had to hold onto the door frame as a loose floorboard wobbled underfoot. The wallpaper was a sludgy green that suggested it had been chosen to hide stains, the mattress seemed to be stuffed with cabbages. The curtains were too small for the window, and the drawers beside the bed didn't shut properly.

An inarticulate sound behind Randolph made him turn to see a pile of sheets and blankets walking around on Dottie's legs. He guided her inside and removed the top layer, unblocking her view.

"Sorry," she said, dumping everything on the bed. "The furniture's a bit...a bit..."

"Yes, it is," Randolph said with feeling.

"Jack buys it secondhand, you see. Never mind. It's clean, I see to that."

"I believe you. Let me help you make up the bed."

This wasn't a success, except that his efforts reduced Dottie to tears of laughter. "I'll do it," she said when she'd recovered. "It'll be quicker."

She proceeded to attack the bed in a wild frenzy of efficiency, punching seven bells out of the pillows until they took on some sort of shape.

"I still feel I should atone for making your life difficult," he said. "Let me take you for a meal."

"But you've just had a meal."

He looked at her.

"No, I suppose not," she sighed. "You didn't really touch it, did you? But you don't have to—"

"I should like to. Please." When she hesitated he

added shamelessly, "Just think of Brenda making up to your fiancé."

"Right," she said, setting her chin firmly. "Let's go."

At his suggestion she used his mobile to call a cab to collect them in Hanver Street.

"Why Hanver Street?" he asked. "Is this a pedestrians only area?"

"No, but cabs don't like coming here because of all the one-way streets," she explained as they stepped outside. "Hanver Street is just on the other side of Hanver Park."

The little park was at the end of the road. A tiny place, just a stretch of greenery, a few swings and a little wood, it was an unexpected delight in this dingy neighborhood. It lay on a gentle slope, and as they descended the broad steps Randolph's attention was taken by two figures on the grass verge. They wore black jeans and sweaters. Their hair was completely covered by black woolly hats, and their faces were painted dead-white. Silent and mysterious, they were gravely miming a little scene. Their manner was gentle, and occasionally they smiled at the odd passerby who stopped to regard them. They might have been young men or young women. It was impossible to tell.

Randolph took out some coins, but the two performers threw up their hands in horror, seeming genuinely shocked.

"You don't want money?" Randolph asked.

As one, they laid their right hands over their hearts and bowed graciously, as if to say that it was their pleasure to give. Randolph was charmed. He would have watched them longer but Dottie had seen their cab at the far gate, and seized his hand.

Her eyes widened when he gave the driver their destination.

"I can't go to The Majestic," she said, scandalized. "It's posher than the Ritz. I've never been anywhere like that before."

"Then it's time you did."

"Don't be daft, I can't go like this."

"Get in," he said, taking her arm and urging her into the cab.

It swept them away from the dreary surroundings and off to central London, where the store windows shone and the restaurants glittered. Dottie pressed her nose to the window, eyes shining in a way that made Randolph wonder how often she had any kind of treat.

He'd discovered so many new things that day that he regarded his horizons as fully enlarged, and was beginning to think there was no more for him to learn.

He was wrong.

The Majestic offered him an experience that he'd never known before and if he never knew it again until his last day on earth it would still be too soon.

As they pulled up before the luxurious restaurant the cab door was opened by a doorman in an extravagant livery. He bowed, his face wreathed in obsequious smiles that vanished when he saw Dottie.

"I am very sorry, sir," he said, addressing Randolph as if Dottie wasn't there, "the restaurant has a dress code. Ladies must wear skirts."

The habit of years made Randolph say impatiently, "Nonsense."

"I'm afraid the rule cannot be broken, sir."

Only a lifetime of thinking before he spoke stopped him announcing who he was. Prince Randolph went where he pleased and restaurant owners groveled for his patronage. Now he was being told that he wasn't good enough, or rather, his friend wasn't good enough. The sight of Dottie's face gave him a nasty shock. She was smiling, but not in her normal joyous way. This smile had a forced brightness that told him she was hurt.

He was suddenly full of anger but it was directed at himself. She'd tried to warn him and he'd ridden roughshod over her.

"Come on," he said, taking her arm gently. "This place doesn't suit our requirements. We'll find somewhere better, that does."

That made the doorman swell like a turkey.

Dottie walked along the street in silence. Randolph was about to say something comforting when she began to laugh. "His *face!*"

"It was worth seeing," he admitted. He was thinking of some women he knew who would have said, "I told you so," and sulked until they thought he'd been punished enough.

Being offended was the last thing on Dottie's mind. She was in seventh heaven, enjoying the first fun outing she'd had in years. She recalled the last time she'd been in London's glamorous West End, as a child, when Grandad had brought her to see Santa Claus in one of the stores.

This felt much the same. The way her companion had whisked her away and brought her to this glittering street gave him much in common with Santa. Of course he was young for the part, and far too handsome, but she clung to the analogy because it left her free to admire him without feeling guilty about Mike.

They found somewhere a little farther along, different from The Majestic in every way except for its prices, which were even higher. This was an emporium of nouvelle cuisine, bright, modern, chic, sexy.

"All right for us to come in?" Randolph asked the man in jeans and shirt leaning against the door.

"You got the bread, man?" He indicated the exorbitant prices.

"He's got the bread," Dottie said, seeing Randolph's baffled expression.

"Bread?" he asked as they made their way to the table.

"Money." A horrid thought struck her. "You *have* got the bread, haven't you?"

"I think I can manage a loaf or two."

The waiter led them to a table by the window, through which they could catch a glimpse of the River Thames. He pulled out a chair for Dottie, who seemed disconcerted.

"I can't sit down," she protested to Randolph. "He's holding it too far away."

"Just sit," he advised. "Trust him, he'll move it into place as your legs bend."

She tried, and seemed relieved when she landed safely.

"Obviously you don't know the story of the Empress Eugenie," Randolph said, amused.

"Who was she?"

"She lived in the middle of the nineteenth century, and married the French emperor Napoleon III. But she was a *parvenu.*"

"A *what?*"

"An upstart. She wasn't born royal. She had to learn. In her memoirs she told how she and her husband once shared a box at the opera with Queen Victoria, and when they sat down she looked behind her to see the chair. But Victoria didn't look back. She *knew* the chair would be in place, because for her it always had been. Eugenie said that was when she understood the difference between a true royal like Victoria, and a parvenu like herself."

"I know how she feels," Dottie said. "Life's always waiting to kick the chair away. Now me, I'd just fall straight on my ass."

Randolph winced.

"You sound like Brenda," Dottie continued. "She's got a thing about royalty. Just now she keeps on talking about Elluria and how they've lost their king 'cos he's illegitimate, or some such thing."

"How did she know that?" Randolph asked quickly.

"This magazine she reads, *Royal Secrets.* All the dirt."

And the magazine would certainly have contained a picture of himself, he realized. He could only be grateful for the plastic palm in the café that had prevented Brenda from seeing him well enough to blow his cover.

"Do you also read *Royal Secrets?*" he asked apprehensively.

"Not me. Well, it's all cobblers, isn't it?"

"Cobblers?" he asked, his eyes starting to glaze.

"Rubbish. Royalty! Who needs it these days?"

"What about the British royal family?"

"Oh look, I don't mean them any harm," Dottie explained hurriedly. "I don't want to see them exterminated or anything—just pensioned off."

The waiter was hovering expectantly. After studying the menu with bafflement Dottie accepted Randolph's suggestion that he order for her.

"Do you have any preference about wine?" he asked, knowing the answer.

"A half of beer will do me," she said.

"I'm not sure that they do beer. How about—?" He named a French wine, not telling her that it cost nearly one hundred pounds a bottle, and Dottie smiled and said she guessed that would do.

When the food arrived she made slow progress because she seemed unable to talk without gesticulating, and her hands were seldom free to eat. But after a while she seemed to be enjoying herself.

"You're not English are you?" she said between mouthfuls. "You've got a funny voice. No, I mean—not funny exactly..."

"It's all right," he said, rescuing her. "I do have an accent." He tried to sound casual. "Actually, I come from Elluria."

"What, that place we were just talking about?"

"The very same."

"Cor! Fancy that!" She giggled. "You're not royal, are you?"

"No," he said quietly. "I'm not."

It was true, he told his conscience. It had been true for several weeks now.

"I don't know anything about Elluria," she admitted. "Not even where it is."

"It's in the center of Europe. It's quite small, about three million people. The traditional language is German, but everyone speaks English as well because it's the language of trade and tourism, and these are important to us."

"Is that why you're here?"

"In a sense. You might say that I've come on a fact-finding expedition."

"But why Wenford? Why The Grand? You're completely out of place there."

"Thank you."

"Sorry, I didn't mean to be rude. I speak first and think later. Always have, and I guess I always will. Too late to change now."

"Don't you think you could try?" Randolph ventured.

She gave a worried little frown. "Are you mad at me?"

"No, speaking first and thinking later is charming in a young woman, but there are times and situations when it could be damaging."

"You mean when I'm an ugly old battle-ax?" she asked cheerfully, spreading her hands wide and forcing a waiter to swerve around her.

"I can't imagine that you could ever be ugly," he said truthfully.

"But a battle-ax, right? Mike says it's like being with a dictator sometimes."

"And you don't mind him saying things like that?"

She chuckled. "Oh, if he steps out of line I just give him a long, lingering kiss, and then he forgets everything else."

That was wise of her, he thought. A kiss from those lips wouldn't just be about sex. It would be about laughter and sunshine, wine, sweetness and all the good things of life.

"Guys never give me any trouble," she added blithely.

"You give them all long, lingering kisses?" he asked, startled.

"No need. A smile usually does it. But you're quite right. The day'll come when they're not trying to get me into bed—"

"Would you mind keeping your voice down?" he begged, conscious of the waiter just behind her.

"And then I'll have to watch my mouth," she finished.

He reddened. "That's not really what I said."

"Well, it's what you meant by 'damaging.' Me coming out with something daft isn't going to damage anyone but me, now is it? Kingdoms aren't going to rise and fall because Dottie Hebden opened her big gob—"

"Aren't they?" he murmured grimly.

"—and that's lucky because she's always blurting out something stupid. A really daft cow, that's what everyone says. Well, Mike doesn't say it because he doesn't dare but...oh heck, I'm sorry!"

"It's perfectly all right," said the waiter, rubbing himself down. Carried away by her own eloquence, Dottie had made a wildly expansive gesture right across his path. He'd gone straight into it before he could stop, with disastrous consequences to the artistic creation in his hands.

A wail from behind him indicated that the chef had arrived on the scene, and it wasn't all right with him. "My masterpiece," he moaned, regarding the mess on the floor.

"I shall naturally pay for any damage," Randolph declared with a touch of loftiness. It was maddening to have this interruption when he was getting a glimpse into Dottie's mind, even though what he found there made him deeply apprehensive.

"Damage? Damage?" shrilled the chef. "It took me an hour to get it perfect. Do you really think that you can—?"

"I never think," Dottie said penitently. "Oh, I'm so sorry. How could you ever forgive me?"

She'd risen from the table and taken the chef's hands in hers, smiling up into his eyes. He was a foot taller, so that Randolph was able to see straight over Dottie's head, and observe the precise effect she was having on the man. From avenging angel to trembling jelly in three seconds flat, he thought in admiration. The chef was almost burbling, assuring her that there would be no further trouble, she wasn't to worry herself...

"That was very clever," he said when they were alone again. "How long did it take you to perfect it?"

"Hey, c'mon, I wasn't being cynical." Her tone suggested a crime.

"Be fair. You were just boasting about how you could reduce Mike to a quivering wreck any time you liked—"

"I was not boasting," she said firmly. "Mike *loves* me, which is why it works."

"With him, maybe, but what about the others? 'A smile usually does it,' is what you said. You knew exactly what you were up to just then, Dottie."

"Oh well." She gave a wicked chuckle. "I didn't do badly, did I?"

"No, they're not even going to charge for the 'masterpiece' you ruined. One flash of your eyes and he buckled at the knees."

"But that's not being cynical," she said earnestly. "That's being nice to people. I did spoil his masterpiece, so I just said sorry and...and...that's all there was to it.''

She meant it, he realized. Dottie might talk about playing off her tricks, but the truth was she preferred being nice to people. The smile sprang from her kindness and honesty, which was why it was dynamite.

Encouraged by Randolph, Dottie chatted about her family, which seemed almost nonexistent. Neither her parents nor her grandparents were still alive, and he gathered that she'd been alone since she was sixteen. She told this part of the tale without conscious pathos. She'd fended for herself and survived with her humor intact. No big deal.

She knew how to tell a funny story, and a woman who could do that had never been part of Randolph's experience. All the strains and tensions of his life seemed to fall away as he rocked with laughter at her description of her grandmother coping with her grandfather's numerous flirtations.

```''Course she knew he loved her really, and she loved him, but she was always chucking pans at him, and if she really thought he'd blotted his copybook she'd be after him like a ferret up a drainpipe.''

``Pardon me?'' he said, startled. ``Ferret? Drainpipe?'' These too, were outside his experience.

``Sorry. Don't suppose you've ever seen a ferret, have you?''

``No,'' he said thankfully.

``Grandpa wanted to keep some, as pets, but Grandma said over her dead body, and he said not to tempt him.''

She finished the meal with an exotic ice cream and another glass of wine.

``It's my third,'' she said guiltily. ``Ought I?''
```

"Wine as good as this can be drunk safely," he assured her. "And I promise you're quite safe with me."

"No funny business?"

"No funny business."

The word, "pity," flitted through her head and was gone before she could be sure it had ever been there. The man across the table was regarding her with kindly amusement. His eyes were warm and suddenly she felt as though the two of them were the only people left in the world. She wondered why she hadn't realized before just how handsome he was.

She seemed to see him more clearly than before, and it occurred to her that he was two different men. He had the body of an athlete, broad shouldered, tall and powerful, as though his whole frame had been made hard and taut by a life in the outdoors. His hands were a rare combination of size and grace, as though he could hold anything in them, with no appearance of effort.

Yet his face told a different story. It was lean, almost austere, with fine features and dark, expressive eyes: the face of a thinker, a scholar, perhaps a poet. This was something Dottie had never seen in her life before, yet she recognized it at once, and felt a faint stir of response.

Then she laughed at herself. What could she do with a man like this? A man she couldn't read.

"Are you a soldier?" she asked impulsively.

"Why do you ask?"

"Just...something about you," she said helplessly. Life in a family with a small vocabulary hadn't left her equipped for this.

"I did a stint in the army," he said truthfully. It had been part of his training.

"But not anymore? I mean, you didn't want to make a career of it?"

"No, but it's not impossible that I might return," he said with a wry grimace. She made no answer and he saw a vague look in her eyes, as though she had gone into a trance. "Dottie?"

She came back to earth. She'd been watching his mouth, the way the lips moved against each other as he spoke, or used them expressively.

"Yes?"

"What were you thinking?"

"That this is the best night out I've ever had."

"Doesn't Mike take you out?"

"Yes, we go dog racing sometimes. It's great."

"What do you want, Dottie?" he asked suddenly. "I mean, out of life."

"But you know what I want. I'm going to marry Mike and we're going to have the garage."

"And live happily ever after," he finished wryly. "Nothing else?"

"Lots of kids."

"But don't you ever want to soar into the heavens?"

"In an airplane? With me it was always boats."

"How do you mean?"

"Grandpa used to take me to see the River Thames. I loved it. I watched the boats and thought about faraway places." She glanced through the window to where the river flowed, shining under the shore lights and those from the occasional boat.

"Why don't you show me?" Randolph suggested, signaling to the waiter.

In minutes they were outside, making their way toward the water. It was quiet along the embankment, and they could hear the soft lap of the water. For a while Dottie had nothing to say, until at last she rested her arms against the stone ledge overlooking the river with a sigh of deep contentment.

"I didn't really mean soaring in an airplane, Dottie," Randolph said, taking up the thread of their previous conversation. "I meant, inside you."

"People don't soar in Wenford," she said with a faint sigh. "It's not a soaring sort of place."

"But what about the 'faraway' you mentioned? What about the lands of your dreams? Don't you ever have dreams? You've got your café and your garage mechanic, and that's it?"

"You're having a go at poor Mike, aren't you? Look, I know he's not the answer to every maiden's prayer—"

"That depends what you think the maiden was praying for," he said wryly.

She gave a choke of laughter. "Well, this maiden was praying for someone who was kind and good-natured, and who'd let her look after him."

"That's what you like? Looking after people?"

"Of course," she said, sounding surprised, as though it was a matter of course. "It's wonderful to be needed. I used to think—"

"Go on," he said when she stopped.

"You mustn't laugh."

"I promise."

"Well, at first I wanted to be an actress. But then I used to think I'd like to be a children's nurse."

"Why would I laugh at that?"

"Well, honestly! Me! I'm too dumb. I never passed any exams at school. In fact I never took any. There was just me and Grandpa by then and he was always sick so I bunked off school.''

''But that doesn't mean you're dumb, just caring. If there'd been someone to care for you, you'd have done well.''

''I did have someone to care for me,'' she said firmly. ''Grandpa loved me. It's just that things got on top of him a bit. Anyway, I couldn't be a nurse. It's not in my stars.''

''You read horoscopes?''

''No, not that sort of stars.'' In a sudden expansive gesture she flung a hand up to the night sky. ''Fate,'' she said dramatically. ''Destiny. There's a niche waiting for you somewhere in the world, that only you can fill.''

He'd once thought the same. His niche had been clear, and he was well prepared for it. But then it had turned out not to be his at all. ''That's a dangerous doctrine,'' he said somberly.

She sighed and went back to gazing over the water. ''You're right. It's not good to dream too much. It's better to be a realist.''

''Maybe reality will turn out to be stranger than you think,'' he murmured.

She looked at him. ''You sound as though that meant something particular.''

''Nothing special,'' he said hastily, trying to make his face and voice blank so that his pain wouldn't show. Mostly he kept that pain under stern control, but this disconcerting young woman had touched a nerve.

A cab rumbled by and he hailed it. ''Let's go back,'' he said.

The lamps were still on in Hanver Park, and as they

climbed the broad steps Randolph became aware of something very curious. But for themselves the park was empty, yet the two mime artists were still there, earnestly gesticulating, oblivious to the fact that nobody was watching them. They seemed completely happy in a world of their own, where no audience was needed.

They stopped to watch. The entertainers continued in serene silence, their white faces ghostly under the lamps. After a while Randolph looked away from them, to Dottie.

She was entranced, oblivious to him, her eyes gleaming with the colored lamps, her lips parted in a half smile of delight. He wondered when he'd last been so happily unselfconscious, but he couldn't remember it. Perhaps never.

Dottie's radiant innocence was like a blow to his heart. She was so candid and trusting, so sure the rest of the world was as honest as herself. How could she realize that the man with her was the serpent in Eden, plotting to destroy her happiness? He would take everything away, first the world in which she was at ease, then the lover who meant so much to her. And in their place he offered wealth, grandeur and a kind of power—all of which, Randolph was increasingly convinced, would mean nothing to her.

She looked up at him suddenly. "What's the matter?"

"Nothing. Nothing's the matter."

"Yes it is. You were thinking about something that made you sad."

Her shrewdness caught him off guard and for a moment he floundered.

"Is it me?" she asked. "Have I done something wrong?"

"No Dottie," he said gently. "You've done nothing wrong. You've been delightful, all evening."

The two artists had stopped miming and were watching them intently, looking from him to her, and back.

"Yeah, well, I gave you a laugh, anyway."

"More than that," he said seriously. "I think you're one of the nicest people I've ever known."

A soft breeze had sprung up, making her hair drift about her face. Randolph couldn't take his eyes from her.

"It's been a lovely, lovely evening," she sighed. "Like magic."

"Yes. A kind of magic. That's just what it was."

Dottie became aware of the anxious gaze from the two white faces. "What's up with you two?"

"I think they want me to kiss you," Randolph said, and putting his fingers under her chin, he lifted it and bent his head.

He made no attempt to put his arms around her, and his lips barely touched hers. It wasn't passion that she felt in him, but tenderness, a continuation of the enchantment that had pervaded the whole evening. When he lifted his head he saw that she was smiling. He smiled back, then, turning to the two mimes he said, "Thank you."

Their response was to jump for joy, dancing around Dottie and Randolph. He took some money out and again tried to give it to them. "Won't you let me show my gratitude?"

But, as before, they shook their heads. Then they

turned and ran away, hand in hand, until they vanished into the darkness of the trees.

"Why did you thank them?" Dottie asked, speaking as in a dream.

"Because without them I wouldn't have dared to kiss you."

"I'm glad they wouldn't take money," Dottie said. "That would have spoiled it somehow."

"Yes," he said, in quick appreciation. "It would."

Dottie didn't say anything, but stood looking at him in unutterable content. This was part of the glory of the whole evening. It was as though time had been suspended for a few hours. Later it would start again and she would become her real self once more. But nothing would be quite the same.

They wandered on out of the park until they reached the hotel, which was in darkness.

"Got your key?" she asked.

"Later. I'm walking you home."

"It's only two streets away."

"A gentleman doesn't let a lady walk home alone."

And the spell could last a little longer, she thought happily. They walked the two streets in silence and stopped outside a shabby brick house, three floors high.

"Good night, Dottie. Thank you for a lovely evening."

"It should be me thanking you. I've never—" she laughed and sought for words. "I've just never…just never…"

"Never drunk white burgundy?" he said, smiling. "Never eaten nouvelle cuisine?"

"Never talked like that," she said. "It was nice to fly."

"Don't you want to keep on flying?"

She shook her head. "But it was nice to do it once."

"You're so certain that it will never happen again?"

He thought for a moment that she would answer, but then she backed off like someone who'd seen danger. "I've got a real life to live. You can't do that flying."

"But—"

"I have to go in now," she said hurriedly. "Good night." She ran up the short path to the front door.

"Good night," he said regretfully and turned away. But before he'd gone more than a few steps she called out to him. "Yes?" he said hopefully.

"Don't forget to miss a step as you go into your room. Otherwise you'll hit the wobbly floorboard."

"I'll remember."

"Have a good night, and I'll bring you a real English breakfast in the morning."

"Thank you," he said, trying to conceal his feelings at the prospect of this treat. "Good night."

Just before she went to sleep Dottie spoke to a photo of Mike that she kept by her bed. She often did this, and not for the world would she have admitted that it could be more rewarding than talking to the real man.

"It was just a meal—not an actual date or anything—a bit like being taken out when you were a kid. It's not like I fancied him. Well, maybe just a bit…all right, a lot. Okay, Okay, so he kissed me.

And I wouldn't have minded if he'd done it again. But you're the one I love. Honest. Anyway, what were you up to with Bren?"

She turned out the light.

Chapter Three

Thursday was the great day of the week, the day when Dottie finished work early, and met Mike in the park. As two o'clock neared she hurried away from the café, rejoicing in the knowledge that all was right with the world. The sun was shining and heaven, in the shape of a chunky garage mechanic, was just around the corner. The fantasies of the night before were no more than colored dreams, like being taken to the movies. It was easier to think like this because there'd been no sign of Mr. Holsson this morning. She'd done him a good English breakfast, as promised, but had persuaded Jack to take it up.

She entered the little wood that fringed the park, and at first she had to stop and blink as the trees blotted out the light. Then her sight cleared and she realized that she wasn't alone. A man stood leaning against a tree, only half-visible through the slanting sunbeams.

Today he was in slacks and shirt, with the sleeves rolled up past his elbows. He didn't see Dottie at first and she was able to study him, trying to recapture the way he'd seemed the previous evening. But in the morning light she saw only a man whose arms were heavy with muscles, and whose torso beneath the light shirt was lean and hard.

Last night he'd kissed her, but only softly, on the lips. He hadn't put those strong arms around her or drawn her against him. Of course it was better that he hadn't, but for a moment her head spun with the thought. Behind the gentleness of his mouth she'd sensed something else, a tension, an urgency, even an anger, that she'd never known before in a man's kiss.

Her experience was limited: overeager boys whose wishes had exceeded their skill, and whom she'd had to put firmly in their place. And Mike, well-meaning and affectionate, always glad to please her.

But now she'd encountered something different, not a boy but a man, with the power to excite her mysteriously. She closed her eyes, and when she opened them again something had changed. The sun struck him at an angle that made him seem enclosed in a golden light, and for a moment it was like seeing an apparition; a benevolent apparition that hinted at a glorious future that might tantalize her for a moment before vanishing.

He looked up to where she stood. But although his eyes were fixed on her she had a feeling that it wasn't herself he was looking at, but someone else. The impression was so strong that she turned to look behind her. But then he smiled, and she knew it was just for her.

Randolph had awoken with a strange sensation, as though the new world he'd glimpsed last night was still there, inviting him to enter again, because she was there. She had the gift of spring, he thought, and was startled at himself, because such a poetic thought had never crossed his mind before. All his training urged him to avoid such ideas, but when he saw her again he smiled despite himself.

"Was your breakfast all right?" she asked, coming closer to him. "You didn't eat it all."

He nearly said frivolously, "That was because you didn't bring it up to me." But he pulled himself together. He was here on serious business.

"It was excellent," he said, "but a little more than I normally eat. The tea was—" he hunted for the word, "very strong," he said at last.

"Round here we say tea's not tea unless you can stand the spoon up in it."

"So I gathered," he said with feeling.

It was better to keep the talk light, and so avoid the swirling undercurrents.

"Are you exploring the neighborhood?" she asked as they fell into step.

"No, I was waiting for you."

The sudden gravity in his voice made Dottie's heart beat faster, as though she was faced with unknown danger.

"I warned you about that floorboard," she said quickly. "If you want to complain—"

"I have no complaints," he said, taking hold of

her arm to halt her. "There are things we need to talk about. Last night—"

"Last night was lovely but..." she shrugged helplessly, "it was last night. Today I'm me again."

"And who were you then?"

"I don't know. Someone I'd never met before. Someone who could fly." Meeting his eyes she saw an understanding that disconcerted her. It was as though he knew everything she would say before she'd thought of it herself. It made her laugh self-consciously. "Whoever she was, it's time she went her way and let me go mine."

"Was she the one who kissed me?"

"She didn't," Dottie said, trying to be firm. "It was you... Oh, I don't know anything anymore."

"I've been a bit confused myself," he admitted. "But I think it was something like this."

He leaned swiftly down and laid his mouth over hers. He knew there was danger in it, because springtime was always dangerous to a man who'd never known it before. But his caution had deserted him. He must kiss this one woman or regret the loss all his life.

He'd moved too swiftly for Dottie to prevent him. She instinctively put her hand up, but it merely fell on his shoulder. He almost seemed to be hypnotizing her so that her will died away, and she could do only what he was telling her. Obeying those silent instructions, she failed to protest when he put his hands gently on either side of her face.

She hadn't known that a man's lips against hers could feel like this, tender and coaxing, yet impossible to deny. She had a strange feeling that she was kissing him with all of her, not just her mouth. Certainly all of her was responding, from the top of her head, down the length of her suddenly tingling body, right to her curling toes.

Her hands had become rebellious. They wanted to rove over his body, across the hard muscles of his arms and chest and discover the flatness of his stomach, the power of his thighs. She knew that these things were true about him because the movements of his mouth against hers were silently telling her.

Somewhere in her consciousness doors and windows opened wide, showing vistas of far horizons, stormy seas, endless blue skies. The world was so much bigger than she'd dreamed, and was full of so many unsuspected things. There was exploring to do, and it would take her far beyond the comfortable little world in which she'd planned to contain herself and Mike—

Mike!

The word was like a thunderclap in Dottie's brain. Shocked at herself, she drew sharply back and stared at him. Then she wrenched herself out of Randolph's arms and ran deeper into the wood.

"Dottie!" he called and ran after her. "Don't go, please. I'm sorry, I didn't mean to offend you."

"No," she said, turning back to him and managing a shaky laugh. "This is so silly. It's just…just…"

"Spring makes people do silly things," he said hastily. "I got carried away."

"You?" she echoed with such naïve astonishment that he had no doubt how he looked to her: a man who couldn't let himself be spontaneous. And she was right. When had it last happened? Never before he met her.

"Perhaps it's because I'm a tourist," he improvised. "People go mad when they travel abroad—"

"And they make other people mad too," she agreed, frantically rewriting history. She was in love with Mike, so she hadn't kissed this man. At least, she *had* but she hadn't really enjoyed it—not as much as she thought she had.

"I have to go now," she said. "It was nice seeing you again but—" suddenly the words came out in a gabble, "I really must go."

She rushed away without a backward glance, eager to find Mike and the safe, cozy world she knew with him. There was nothing safe or cozy about this stranger. He made her think of lightning and fire, and she needed to get away from him.

Just beyond the trees she found Mike sitting on a wooden bench, munching a sandwich. He was startled out of his contented reverie by Dottie's arms about his neck as she flung herself down beside him.

"Careful, Dot," he protested. "You'll get peanut butter over me."

The last words were lost in the most fervent kiss she'd ever given him. He abandoned the sandwich and embraced her back, despite his surprise.

"Have you been taking something?" he demanded when he could breathe.

"Yes, I'm drunk with spring," she said idiotically. "And I wanted—" she took a deep breath, "the most wonderful kiss in the world."

"And you reckoned I could give you that?" Mike asked, awed. "Eee, Dot!"

"Of course. Who else? You're the one I love."

She said this so fiercely that Mike stared at her in alarm. Randolph, a short distance away, behind a tree, couldn't see him clearly, but he could sense the reaction. What did Mike understand of a woman like this? In the few moments it had taken him to brush his mouth against Dottie's he had discovered the banked fires of passion waiting for the one man to bring it forth. And that man wasn't this well meaning oaf, whatever she believed.

Her next words gave him a nasty shock.

"Mike, when are we going to set the date?"

"Whenever you like, Dot. But I thought we decided to wait until we had the deposit for the garage."

"I've changed my mind. I'm going to snap you up fast, before Bren gets her claws into you."

"Aw, c'mon. You know I love you Dot. I couldn't care about anyone else, any more than you could."

Dottie's voice was suddenly high and breathless. "Of course we couldn't, but let's not take chances. You—you never know what's going to happen."

"All right. Whatever you say."

"No, it shouldn't be just what I say. It should be what *we* say." She sounded suddenly despondent. "Don't you *want* to marry me?"

"Course I do. I said yes when you proposed, didn't I? All right, don't hit me."

From behind the tree Randolph could hear a scuffle and laughter that ended very suddenly. He resisted the impulse to lean out and see what was happening, but the silence went on longer than he liked.

"Are we going to have a honeymoon?" Mike asked at last.

"Sure. How about a Caribbean cruise?"

"Yeah, I'd like one of them."

"Price no object," Dottie said grandiloquently.

"Three thousand, four thousand, or there's a top flight cruise at seven thousand."

"Let's have that," Mike said. "Only the best for us."

"Luxury class."

"Money to burn."

"Our every whim catered for," she cried to the blue sky.

"We'll eat off gold plates."

Hand in hand, they considered this for a moment.

"Unless you'd prefer a month in Hawaii," Dottie offered.

"Is that the one where you get sexy maidens meeting you on the beach with garlands?"

"On second thought, forget Hawaii."

Mike gave his easygoing chuckle. "Anything you say, Dot." He squeezed her hand as they left the brightly colored dreams behind. "Mind you, if you go off the cruise idea, Uncle Joe's always said we could borrow his caravan for a long weekend."

"That would be lovely," Dottie said.

She sounded as enthusiastic about the cheap caravan as the luxury cruise that existed only in her lively imagination, and Randolph had to admire her spirit. It might be nice for a man to share his life with such a funny, gutsy lady. It was the same spirit that he admired in Sophie, he reminded himself. Not that Sophie's lofty mind would have indulged in that crazy fantasy.

With regret he remembered that Dottie's fantasies too, must be dispelled. He had lingered as long as he dared. Now it was time to claim her for his country, and her duty. He stepped out from behind the tree, treading on a twig, its snap making Dottie look up quickly.

"Are you following me?" she demanded.

Then Randolph, the severe and practical man, was truly inspired.

"Yes," he said. "I am following you—both of you. I had to be sure that you were suitable for the prize. A stay in a luxury hotel as guests of the Ellurian gov—tourist authority."

"Elluria?" Dottie echoed, wrinkling her brow. "That's the place you were telling me about."

"We're trying to promote it as somewhere to take the vacation of a lifetime," Randolph said. "It's never been done before, which is why so few people think of traveling there. But we have everything, magnificent scenery, great art, history—"

"Disneyland?" Mike asked eagerly.

"No," Randolph was forced to admit, "we don't have Disneyland. But we have Lake Bellanon, with its beautiful beaches. I think you'll both like it there."

"Us?" Dottie asked suspiciously.

"It's been my task to find two people who would make best use of the prize. It has to be a young couple, so that as well as enjoying our hospitality you can tell us what Elluria needs to attract other young people. It will be everything you've dreamed of—money to burn, gold plates, your every whim catered for."

If only, he thought, Mike didn't say, "Eee, Dot!" But he did. Randolph ground his teeth.

"It's too good to be true," Mike went on.

"Right! Too good to be true," Dottie said, showing an astuteness that dismayed Randolph. "In real life, things just don't get handed to you on a plate like this. I'm suspicious."

"He can't be stocking a harem, Dot," Mike pointed out. "Not if he wants me as well."

"You don't know that. He's probably covering all the angles."

"Pardon?"

"Never mind," she said hastily. Randolph's lips were twitching. He'd divined her meaning at once, while Mike was still floundering around trying to believe she'd meant what he thought she'd meant.

"I promise you, it's all on the level," Randolph said smoothly. "Wouldn't you like a free vacation, spending money, new wardrobe?"

Dottie drew a long breath at the thought of new clothes, but she was torn two ways, trying to equate this with his behavior to her earlier. Randolph understood her perfectly and his conscience smote him.

"It could be our honeymoon," she said at last.

"No," Randolph said hastily, "we have to leave at once."

"But if we got a special license..."

Seeing disaster staring him in the face Randolph became even more inspired.

"I must make a confession, Ms. Hebden. The fact is that you two are replacements. The original prize winners had to drop out at the last minute. The celebrations are all arranged. When I return to Elluria tonight I must take you with me or I'll probably lose my job."

"Tonight?" Dottie squealed. "And what about *our* jobs?"

"I promise to settle everything with your employers. The Ellurian tourist authority will provide temporary replacements, at their own expense. Generous expense. Your employers will gain on the transactions.''

''But we don't have passports,'' Dottie pointed out.

''You will travel on Ellurian diplomatic passports.''

''A whole month's free vacation,'' Mike mused. ''It's a pity it couldn't have been our honeymoon.''

''But it can,'' Dottie said triumphantly. ''We can get married out there. Think what terrific publicity for tourism that will be.'' She beamed at Randolph. ''You'd like that, wouldn't you?''

''Of course,'' he said in a hollow voice.

It seemed that as he avoided one pitfall another opened at his feet. His conscience was troubling him more every minute. But he had no choice. At all costs, he had to get Dottie to Elluria, or his country would be at Harold's mercy, and that mustn't be allowed to happen.

''We can be married at once,'' Dottie was murmuring, almost to herself. ''Oh but look, it's nonsense. Things don't happen like this. We have to be realistic.''

''Perhaps you can be too realistic,'' Randolph pointed out. ''Take the chance life holds out to you.'' The cunning of the serpent made him add, ''Just think how mad Brenda will be when she finds out! Of course, by then it will be too late.''

''Oh, if only I could be there to see her face,'' Dottie breathed.

''But you won't,'' Randolph reminded her. ''You'll be in Elluria, with Mike.''

''Let's go,'' Dottie said at once. She jumped to her feet, her face shining with joy. ''Oh Mike, Mike!''

She threw her arms about him and they hugged each other exuberantly. Randolph suddenly looked away. When he looked back he found Dottie regarding him, and he could have sworn there was accusation in her eyes.

Like all crown princes of Elluria, Randolph had spent some time in the army. There he'd learned lessons about tactics, strategy and intelligence gathering that stood him in good stead now.

Certain things were simple, like arranging two diplomatic passports. Sorting matters with Mike and Dottie's employers were tasks for embassy attachés. But keeping his two quarries in protective custody without arousing Dottie's suspicions further, demanded the skills of a policeman, a magician and a mother hen, and taxed Randolph's ingenuity to the fullest.

Whatever organizing skills Dottie displaying at the café seemed not to carry over into her personal life. Her packing was an exercise in chaos, and the number of times she stopped to remember, "just one more thing," drove Randolph nearly demented.

Finally she made her appearance dressed for traveling in what she called "comfortable clothes." These turned out to be a pair of short shorts which would give her future prime minister heart failure, were he to see them. Luckily Randolph had prepared for this disaster by having suitable clothing waiting on the aircraft.

At last he had them in a car on the way to the airport, and their attention was occupied by the excitement of the trip.

"What happens when we get there?" Mike asked.

"We get married," Dottie said firmly.

"What, today?"

"It will take a few days for the paperwork to be complete," Randolph said hastily. "In the meantime, why don't we celebrate with champagne?"

He produced glasses and a bottle of Bollinger from the car's mini bar, and the moment slid past. At the airport they were whisked through their passport checks with the minimum of fuss, and then onto the small luxuriously appointed aircraft, with its soft armchairs in a pale biscuit color.

"Where are the other passengers?" Dottie asked.

"You are Elluria's honored guests," Randolph informed her. "This is a special plane, part of our hospitality."

It was, in fact, the royal plane, which had been on standby, ready to leave at his command.

Dottie regarded him wryly. Something about this was all wrong, and she was growing more uneasy by the minute. But once they took off she became entranced with gazing out of the window at the sea, and then the coast as they reached France.

"Hey, look at that," she breathed to Mike. Receiving no answer she turned and found Mike missing.

"He's in the cockpit," Randolph explained, coming to sit beside her. "Knowing that he was interested in things mechanical, the captain invited him."

"You fixed that," Dottie said. It wasn't a question. She already knew that this man was a great fixer.

"Yes," he admitted. "I needed to talk to you alone. Please Dottie, it's very important." Having created his chance he found he couldn't use it, and was silent a long time.

"So important that you can't find the words?" she suggested.

"Exactly that. What I have to tell you is so extraordinary that at first you may not believe it. In fact, you won't believe it."

"If I'm not going to believe it, it doesn't matter what words you use," she said, trying to be helpful.

"Oh it matters. A lot hangs on this. You may blame me for...for various thing—"

"Well, I have a few things to blame you for, haven't I?" she said quietly.

She couldn't name the obscure sense of hurt that had troubled her since this morning. Nor would she say aloud that he'd deluded her with false magic, but the unspoken reproach was there in her eyes, and he colored.

"Please hear me out before you judge me," he said.

When she didn't reply he took out a copy of *Royal Secrets* and put it into her hands. "Read page 8," he said.

Frowning she opened at the page, and the first thing she saw was a large picture, captioned, Prince Randolph, The Deposed Heir.

At first she didn't believe what her eyes told her. It was impossible for this to be the man sitting opposite her. But gradually the truth of the likeness became impossible to ignore.

"But...you're Mr. Holsson."

"I'm afraid he doesn't exist. I am—I was Crown Prince Randolph of Elluria. Until recently I was heir to the throne. Then it turned out that my father had never been properly married to my mother. In short, I am a bastard, and incapable of inheriting."

"But what's that got to do with me?"

"Let's say you did your grandfather an injustice. Those tales weren't just the drink talking. You're a direct descendent of the royal house of Elluria."

"Oh, get away with you. This is a windup, isn't it? Any minute now a bloke's going to start filming me for *Candid Camera.*"

"Dorothea, I am trying to be serious. This is not a 'windup.' Your royal descent goes back over a hundred years, to Duke Egbert, who was the king's brother. He married an English lady and went to live in England. They had one child, Dorothea, who married a man called Augustus Hebden, and you're their great-great-great-granddaughter."

"So we're both called Dorothea. It's a coincidence."

"It occurs in every generation, and we've had two Queen Dorotheas. It's a common name in the Ellurian royal family, and in yours I believe?"

"Well, there was my great Aunt Dot... How did you know?"

"Because I've checked the Hebden family and there's no mistake."

"So if I'm descended from a duke, how come I'm running a greasy spoon?"

"Egbert was a spendthrift. He got through his wife's money, but managed to marry his daughter to a wealthy man on the strength of his royal connections. Then he spent his son-in-law's money, too. After that it was downhill all the way. And you are *not* running a greasy spoon. That's in the past. Now you are Her Royal Highness, Princess Dorothea, heiress to the throne of Elluria, and my fifth cousin."

"We're related?"

"Very distantly."

She stared. "You're serious aren't you? You staged this whole thing—"

"To get you to Elluria. Don't expect me to apologize. Without you the next heir is Harold of Korburg, and it makes me go cold to think of what will happen to my country if he gets his hands on it. Elluria is rich in minerals and Harold is greedy. He would sell the ground out from under us, and spend nothing on the people. You *must* become the queen. Anything else is unthinkable."

"For you, maybe. Who gave you the right to kidnap me?"

"I didn't—"

"Oh yes you did. Don't play word games with me. You talked me onto this plane with a pack of lies."

"Yes, I did," he admitted. "That's how desperate the situation is. Dorothea—"

"Don't call me that. I'm Dottie."

"Not anymore. For the past ten minutes we've been in Ellurian air space, and in this country you are Princess Dorothea."

"Then listen to me, buster. Princess Dorothea demands to see the British consul."

Randolph had grown pale. "Her Royal Highness's commands will be obeyed as soon as we land. In the meantime, I've arranged for some more elegant clothing to be on board. May I suggest that you attire yourself suitably for your first appearance before your people?"

Dottie looked at him and a hint of mulishness crept into her eyes. "You've got a nerve, dictating my clothes for me. I'll arrive as Dottie Hebden, because that's who I am. And if that's not good enough for you, the sooner you send me home, the better pleased I'll be."

A steward appeared and addressed Randolph. "Sir, the captain says we'll be landing in a few moments."

Randolph thanked him, and as soon as he departed said urgently, "There isn't much time. Please put the dress on. I promise you, it'll suit you. And your people will expect you to look the part."

"Meaning that I don't look the part now."

"No," he said, suppressing a shudder.

"Good. Then they won't get any ideas about my staying here. I'll go as I am."

"But Dottie—Dorothea—"

"Dottie will do. Shouldn't Mike be coming back here if we're landing?" She heard Randolph's sound of exasperation and said, "It wouldn't work, honestly. I couldn't carry it off. Giving people orders—"

"Is this the woman who wanted to be 'Authority with a capital *A*'?"

"In that tatty café, yes, but I couldn't give orders in real life."

Before he could reply Mike returned from the cockpit, full of the things he'd seen and eager to share them with Dottie.

"Yes, love," she said kindly. "We'll talk about it later. I want to tell you what this joker's up to." Briefly she outlined what Randolph had told her, but with an ironic tone, managing to imply that only a madman would believe a word of it.

"We're going to be landing in a minute," she said, "and there'll be all sorts going on."

"What are we going to do?" Mike asked.

She took his face between her hands. "Mike darling, don't say anything. Just leave the talking to me.''

As she delivered the order she caught Randolph's ironic eye on her.

To Dottie's relief their arrival passed off quietly. The plane came to rest in a discreet corner of the airfield, steps were rolled up, and she descended, firmly holding onto Mike, straight to a waiting limousine. As soon as Randolph had joined them the journey began.

The light was fading and she could see little through the car's darkened windows. Even so, the sight that met her eyes after twenty minutes was breathtaking.

''That's the royal palace,'' Randolph said, following her gaze.

The classically elegant building was nearly a quarter of a mile long, and was reached by a long avenue of ornate fountains. Two Z-shaped staircases led up the front. Wherever she looked Dottie saw windows filled with faces, proving that her arrival was already known. It was a relief when the car swung around to the side of the building, and a more discreet entrance. To her awe a footman stepped forward and opened her door, bowing slightly.

This was her, Dottie Hebden, being bowed to. Any minute she would wake up.

She allowed Randolph to lead her into the building, and had advanced some yards before she realized something was wrong.

''Where's Mike?'' she demanded.

''My aide is looking after him. I give you my word, he'll come to no harm.''

"As long as he's ready to leave, with me, first thing tomorrow morning," she said with more firmness than she felt.

As he spoke they were rising in a small elevator.

"It's the quickest way up to the state apartments," he explained.

Dottie set her chin but said no more. When the elevator stopped she found herself in a small corridor, with three dark oak doors leading off. Randolph opened the largest.

"This is the rear entrance to your apartment."

She found herself in a set of luxurious rooms that took her breath away. There was the royal reception room, the royal bathroom, the royal dressing room and the royal bedroom. This last one was like a small cathedral, with a ceiling that soared high above them.

"I'll bet this is murder to heat properly," Dottie muttered.

"My mother always said the same thing," Randolph agreed. "That's why you'll be glad of the four poster bed. The drapes keep out drafts. Now, allow me to present your maid, Bertha."

A strongly built young woman with a cheerful face advanced and, to Dottie's horrified fascination, dropped a curtsy. Confused and distracted by this, Dottie obeyed the dictates of good manners and curtsied back. Bertha was aghast.

"I shouldn't have done that, should I?" Dottie muttered.

"Never mind," Randolph whispered back.

"Can't you make her go away?"

"You have Her Royal Highness's permission to leave," Randolph announced, and Bertha fled.

"Now do you believe that this will never work?"

Dottie said in despair when they were alone. "When do I see the British consul?"

"You don't."

"Ahh! I knew it. It's a con."

"Your Royal Highness cannot deal with a mere consul," Randolph explained. "The British ambassador will attend you."

For some reason, that was the moment when she began to believe that this was really happening. The last of her disbelief vanished a few minutes later when the tall, elegant figure of Sir Ambrose Philips entered the room, and bowed to her. He was splendid in evening attire, glittering with ribbons and medals.

"My apologies for not being here earlier," he murmured. "I was attending a dinner."

"I'm sorry I dragged you away from it," she said, suddenly horribly conscious of her shorts.

"On the contrary. I am honored to attend Your Royal Highness." Sir Ambrose gave her a courtly bow.

"I'll leave you now," Randolph said. "I'm sure you'd prefer to talk alone."

As soon as the door had closed on him Dottie whirled on the ambassador. "What's going on here? Do you know?"

"Randolph has apprised me of the situation," he admitted. "I need hardly say how glad Her Majesty's government was to discover that the heir to Elluria hails from the United Kingdom. The understanding between our two countries—"

"Speak English, will you?" she said frantically.

He abandoned his lofty mien. "Elluria is an important country, both in its position and its wealth. Some of the minerals to be found here are as valuable as oil. We have mining agreements that are vital to manufacturing in our country, but Harold of Korburg would tear them up and sell to the highest bidder. He has to be kept out and you're the person to do it.''

''Says who? There must be other heirs.''

''Perhaps there are, but nobody's found them yet. If you walk out, Harold will take over next day.''

''You say that, but I bet I'm not free to leave.''

''You are totally free. But if you leave, your country will suffer.''

''Which one?'' Dottie asked urgently.

''Both of them.''

''And if I stay here, just for a while?''

''Then you would find the British government eager to reward you suitably.''

''Enough to buy a garage?''

''I'm sure there wouldn't be any problem about that.''

She drew a long breath, feeling herself on the brink of an abyss. If only there was someone to hold out a helping hand. But the only face that came into her mind was Randolph's, and she could no longer trust him.

''Oh well,'' she said with a shaky laugh, ''I used to think I'd like to be an actress. It can't be that much different.''

Chapter Four

"May I ask if you've made a decision?" Randolph asked when he returned and found her alone.

"I'm nearly there. What have you done with Mike?"

"He's in his own apartments."

"I want you to take me to him."

"Wouldn't it be better if—"

"Now, please."

"Is this the woman who couldn't give orders?" Randolph asked wryly.

She gave him back gaze for gaze. She understood now that this was a man of whom she must beware. He'd charmed her, but underneath he was pursuing his own agenda, and pursuing it all the more ruthlessly because it was driven by his duty.

"I'm just keeping my end up," she said, defying him with her eyes. "And I need to, otherwise you lot will swamp me. Well, I won't *let* you swamp me. You thought I was an airhead who'd jump on command. Boy were you ever wrong! This is a tough cookie, and you may end up sorry you tangled with me."

"Bravo, Dorothea!" he said at once. "With just such an attitude your ancestors led their people through times of crisis. And those who tangled with them ended up sorry."

"Don't you smooth talk me. It doesn't work. Now let's go and find Mike—if you can remember where you've put him."

"At Your Royal Highness's command."

"I've warned you..."

Instead of leading her to the main door Randolph pressed a tiny knob in the carved panel on one wall, and a door clicked open.

"A secret passage," Dottie breathed, forgetting royal dignity in childish delight.

"Not secret. There are a rabbit warren of these passages linking all the main rooms. It's quicker than going by the public corridors. And, of course, more discreet."

It seemed to Dottie that he led her up hill and down dale before they reached one door that looked exactly like all the others, and Randolph opened it.

"You might have put him a bit closer to me," Dottie observed. "But you weren't taking any chances, were you?"

"No," Randolph said firmly, opening the door. "I wasn't."

They found Mike confronting a splendid dinner, dressed in a silk robe that seemed to swallow him up. He beamed at the sight of Dottie.

"I was wondering where you were, love. This is

grand. Mind you, this place is a bit big for me. I keep getting lost. But we've really fallen on our feet.''

''That's what they want you to think,'' Dottie said urgently. ''But it's all a huge con trick.'' She looked at Randolph, regarding them, took Mike's arm and pulled him into a corner.

''It's not a joke after all. They really think I'm going to be their queen,'' she said in a low voice.

''Get away!''

''That's what I said. But they mean it. Mike, what am I going to do?''

''Well, you don't have to do it if you don't want to, do you? Just tell them no. But not yet. Let's have that holiday we were promised. We're living in grand style.''

''But if we stay too long I might be trapped here.''

''Nah, not you Dot! You always get people jumping to do what you say.''

''Keep your voice down,'' she muttered, conscious of Randolph's sharp ears. ''And it's not true.''

''Yes it is. What about that time—''

''Never mind that,'' she said hastily. ''All right. Just for a while.''

Randolph approached discreetly. ''Why don't we leave Mike to get ready for his night out? Some army officers are eager to entertain him. Good night Mike. Have a pleasant evening.''

Dottie followed Randolph back to her apartment in silence. Once there she asked. ''So what happens next?''

''Some refreshment. And a brief meeting with your chief ministers, at which you can receive their loyal greetings.''

"I can't really do that in shorts, can I?" she conceded with a sigh.

"Your Royal Highness is most gracious."

"Oh no, not you too," she protested. "There's got to be one person here who doesn't talk to me like I'm the fairy on top of the cake. It's Dottie."

"Very well, for the moment—Dottie. Bertha will bring you some clothes, and Aunt Liz will help you with them. She's actually the Countess Gellitz, and I think you'll like her."

The countess arrived a few minutes later. She was middle-aged, motherly and elegant, despite being plump. Dottie was soon calling her Aunt Liz, like everyone else.

The sense of unreality increased when she found herself wearing a simple, elegant white dress, plainly expensive and like nothing she'd ever worn before. Then Bertha got to work on her face and hair while Aunt Liz explained that in future this would be the prerogative of her personal beautician and her personal hairdresser. They must be appointed without delay to prepare her for future big occasions, but as today's meeting was urgent, Bertha would do a "rush job."

To Dottie's awed eyes Bertha's rush job was the equal of the expensive London salons where she'd pressed her nose against the window and dreamed. The woman looking back at her from the mirror had huge, subtly made-up blue eyes, perfectly lined lips and a flawless, peachy complexion. Her eyebrows had mysteriously developed an aristocratic arch, while her short hair had been teased into sophisticated curves.

Obscurely, she could feel herself being transformed into another person, and she tried to cling on to herself, which was hard because she was slipping away. Besides which, the other person looked as if she might be fun to be, and temptation was undermining Dottie's resolve.

I will be strong-minded, she told herself. I will not be seduced by all this. Well—not for long, anyway.

She realized that a dispute was taking place over her head. Aunt Liz had selected gold jewelry, while Bertha preferred diamond-studded platinum. The argument raged while Dottie looked from one to the other like a tennis spectator, ignored by both. Randolph, who'd left the room while she dressed, returned in time to witness the moment.

"I prefer gold," she ventured to say at last.

"You see?" Aunt Liz cried triumphantly. "Her Royal Highness has excellent taste."

Bertha glowered. Dottie mouthed, "Next time" to her

"Well done, Dottie," Randolph murmured. "You have the soul of a diplomat."

At last she stood and regarded her coiffured, manicured, made-up and gilded self in the mirror. There was no doubt that the woman staring back at her looked good. But who was she?

"It's time to meet your ministers," Randolph said.

He positioned her in the middle of her reception room. The double doors were thrown open and a troop of middle-aged men streamed in. Each of them threw her a sharp, curious look before bowing. Randolph introduced them, Jacob Durmand, the prime minister, Alfred Sternheim, chancellor, Felix Andras, minister for Foreign Affairs, Bernhard Enderlin, the minister of the Interior. There were several others, but she lost count.

"Gentlemen," Randolph said gravely, "allow me to present to you Crown Princess Dorothea, heiress to the throne of Elluria."

As he spoke he moved away from her side and joined the men facing her. He was the first to bow, but a little stiffly, as though it came hard to him. Then it hit her. Randolph was openly proclaiming that he was one of her subjects. The thought disconcerted her more than anything else had done in that whole incredible day.

The prime minister stepped forward. "On behalf of your people and your parliament, may I have the honor of welcoming Your Royal Highness..."

It went on for several minutes, during which Dottie pulled herself together and worked out what she was going to say.

At last Jacob Durmand finished and everyone was looking at her expectantly. She took a deep breath.

"I'm grateful to all of you for wanting to make me your queen, but the fact is, it's not on. You're so anxious to find an heir that you've pounced on the first person who looks likely, but there's got to be someone better suited than me. I'm not queen material, honest."

By this time her entire council was staring at her, aghast. Dottie hurried on before she could lose the thread.

"I know you need me around just now, because of Harold. Okay, here's the deal. I'll stay for another few weeks, just to hold the fort against him."

"And when the few weeks are up?" Randolph inquired.

"By then you'll have found another heir. Yes, you will," to forestall their protests she held up her hand in an unconsciously imperious gesture. "You will, because you're going to go on searching. When you've found someone, I'll go home."

"You don't know what you're talking about," Sternheim said scathingly.

Dottie regarded him. "In the meantime I think you should address me as Your Royal Highness," she declared coolly. She then spoiled the effect by muttering to Randolph, "Or do I mean Your Majesty?"

"Not until after your coronation."

"In that case," she told Sternheim, "you should have said, 'You don't know what you're talking about, Your Royal Highness.'"

Sternheim was rendered speechless.

"What are we going to do?" the chancellor groaned.

"We're going to do what our princess suggested," Randolph said.

"You see?" Dottie said sunnily. "I'm right."

"I didn't say you were right," Randolph repressed her. "I said we were going to do it your way—for reasons of realpolitik."

"Pardon?"

"It means you hold all the cards," he said wryly. "But if you're going to be convincing you have to play this for real. As far as the world knows you're here to claim your throne. Let Harold get a hint to the contrary and he'll be at our doors."

"But I don't know how to be a princess."

"At this stage you only have to look like one," Randolph assured her. "Receptions and receiving lines." He added slyly, "The hardest part will be the hours you'll spend being fitted for your new clothes."

"New clothes?" Dottie murmured.

"Your royal dignity demands that you don't wear the same outfit in public twice, so it means a lot of work. But I know you'll do your duty for the sake of the country."

She considered. "Well, if it's my duty, I suppose I might."

"You'll find that—what was that noise?"

"That's the royal stomach rumbling," Dottie muttered. "You promised me something to eat and I haven't had it yet."

"The audience is over," Randolph declared hastily.

Everyone filed out, but Dottie noticed that each man stopped in the doorway to give her a final, doubtful look.

"They know I can't do it," she told Randolph when they were alone.

He whirled on her. "Never, *never* say that," he said fiercely. "Never speak it again, never even think it."

"All right, all right," she said, alarmed by the change in him.

He calmed down. "Forgive me. I didn't mean to shout at you, but this is more important than you can imagine. You must be convinced that you can do it, convinced to your depths. The essence of being a princess is to believe in yourself as a princess. Otherwise how can anyone else believe it?"

She was too tired to argue with him. She watched thankfully as two footmen wheeled in a table, already laid.

"Only for one?" she queried. "Aren't you going to stay?"

"I have urgent business to attend to. You have a

full day tomorrow, so when you've eaten, go straight to bed."

"Your Royal Highness," she reminded him mischievously.

"Go straight to bed, Your Royal Highness."

She climbed into the four poster as soon as she'd eaten, and found it more comfortable than she'd expected. But her thoughts were in too much turmoil for her to sleep, and after lying awake for half an hour she put on the light and began to explore the royal apartments.

The bed could have slept five. It stood on a raised dais that was reached by three steps, so that she had no choice but to look down on the rest of the world, which didn't suit Dottie's ideas at all.

She examined a bookshelf, but its contents were in German, except for a few English magazines about horse breeding. It seemed she had nothing to help her through the long night.

Then she remembered *Royal Secrets.* She'd glanced at the magazine just long enough for Randolph to make his point, then stuffed it into her bag, where it still lay. She pulled it out and curled up in bed for a good read.

It was clearly designed for the semiliterate, which Dottie reckoned was why Brenda read it. Text was kept to a minimum, and pictures covered each page. Many of them were of Randolph, "the dispossessed heir." In flashy accents the magazine described his life. Thirty-two years old, raised to inherit a throne, instructed in military matters, statecraft, diplomacy, then abruptly deposed when his parents' marriage was found to be bigamous.

There were pictures of Randolph as a child, accompanied by a coolly correct looking woman who turned out to be his mother. There he was in his teens, this time with his father, the late King Egbert III, the man who'd so cruelly let him down by making a secret marriage and forgetting about it. Studying his face, easygoing, amiable, weak but lovable, Dottie felt that if she met him in life she would have liked him, even though she, like Randolph, had to suffer for his waywardness.

More pictures: Randolph in army uniform, in white tie and tails, Randolph attending parades, in the royal box at the opera, dancing with a beautiful woman in his arms. The woman was unusually tall, Dottie observed from the dismal depths of five foot one, almost tall enough to look her partner in the eye. The caption said she was Countess Sophie Bekendorf, Prince Randolph's fiancée.

Here the magazine outdid itself, describing the love story in throbbing accents.

> Who can see into the hearts of these lovers, reared to occupy a throne together, now seeing their fortunes shattered? Once a great man in his country, Randolph is now no more than an illegitimate commoner. The Bekendorfs have always raised their daughters to be queens. Will Sophie stay true to the man she loves? Will he hold her to her bargain, or be strong enough to release her?

A strange feeling came over Dottie as she realized that the cardboard cutout in this purple prose was the flesh-and-blood man she'd met in Wenford. This was "Mr. Holsson," who'd helped her make up the bed and laughed at his own awkwardness, who'd charmed her until her head spun.

And all the time he'd known something that she didn't. He'd deceived her. She'd been hurt and angry about that, but now a glimmer of understanding, even sympathy, came to her. What had it been like for him to come and find her, bring her back to Elluria, offer her the throne that was rightfully his? He'd done it smiling, with no hint of what it must have cost him, because it was his duty. For his people he'd sacrificed himself. For their sake he would be no less ruthless in sacrificing her.

Dottie yawned and rubbed her eyes. The clock said two in the morning, and she supposed she ought at least try to sleep. But when she'd turned out the light the room was filled with moonlight, and she couldn't resist going to the window and looking out over the great park that surrounded the palace. The moon picked out the tops of the trees and bushes, and turned the lake into a sheet of silver.

Then she became aware that two figures were walking under the trees beside the lake. One was a tall man whose familiar outline made Dottie grow very still. The other was a woman almost as tall as himself. Together they glided by the water, his arm around her waist, his head bent down toward hers. Dottie watched as they stopped suddenly and turned to each other. She held her breath while there was a sliver of light between the two faces. Then they began walking again, and were soon lost in the blackness of the trees.

Dottie turned away, feeling uncomfortably as though she'd pried into something that was none of her business. After all the new impressions that had assaulted her senses that day, this was one too many.

Leaving the window open, she began to explore again. She'd briefly glimpsed the bathroom before, but now she studied it properly. It was a magnificent creation with a thick cream carpet, elegant tiles and a circular bath sunk into the floor.

"Like Cleopatra," she murmured.

She thought of the bathroom back in Wenford that she shared with five other people, with constant squabbles. The next moment she'd run the water and plunged in. It was bliss and she enjoyed herself for half an hour before emerging to dry herself off on a towel and look around for a bathrobe to snuggle into.

She couldn't see what she wanted, but she caught a glimpse of herself in the tall mirrored doors of the bathroom wardrobe. It was almost the first time she'd seen herself like this, full-length. Both her home and the place where she now lived were too crowded for dancing around naked.

"Hmm!" she murmured, turning slowly, while trying to look over her shoulder. "Pity I'm not taller, but I suppose I'll do."

Not finding a robe, she pulled open one of the doors to the wardrobe. Here too, there was luxury, with the same thick carpet, its own soft lighting, and enough room for her to step inside. She did so, and walked the length, but it was completely empty. She sighed, and decided to go to bed.

Then she discovered a problem....

Randolph was awoken next morning by the sound of someone pounding on the outer door of his apartment. He was sleepily aware of the murmuring of voices, then his valet hurried into the room, his face tense.

"She's gone," he said aghast. "The princess has vanished from her room."

"Impossible," Randolph said testily. "What were the footmen doing?"

"Sir, there have been four footmen outside Her Royal Highness's room all night. They swear she hasn't gone out that way. Nor can she have used the concealed door, because that seems to be locked from the other side."

Randolph knew that this was true, having secured it himself the night before. He'd done the same with the concealed door in Mike's room. He was taking no chances.

He dressed hurriedly and almost ran to the state apartments. Once there he began to be seriously worried. The only possible escape was through the window, which, alarmingly, stood wide open. It was two floors up, and although he told himself that even Dottie wouldn't be crazy enough to escape that way, an inner voice whispered that he had much to learn about her.

He became aware of a flutter among the maids. "What is it now?" he demanded.

"Sir, there's a funny noise coming from the bathroom."

Randolph strode into the bathroom and listened. From behind one of the huge mirrored doors came the unmistakable sound of soft snoring. He pulled open the door and they all stared down at the sight of the crown princess, naked as the day she was born, fast asleep on the floor.

Dottie opened her eyes and favored everyone with her sunniest smile. Randolph instantly tore off his jacket and arranged it around her, throwing a curt dismissal over his shoulder to the interested crowd.

"Dottie," he said, controlling himself, "why are you sleeping on the floor in the—in here? I assure you, it isn't the custom."

"Ouch," she said, moving her stiff limbs gingerly. "Help me up." She reached up her hands and he took them, drawing her gently to her feet while trying not to let the jacket become dislodged. It slipped and he only managed to keep it in place by pulling her against him. To his relief everybody had now left.

"Go and put something on," he commanded in a tight voice. "I'll join you in a minute."

He needed that time to himself to shut out the vision of her entrancing nakedness. She was daintily made and completely perfect, slender but rounded, with cheeky uptilted breasts that he had to fight to exclude from his mind. It was even harder to ignore the fleeting sensation of her enchanting little body pressed against his own.

Only when he was sure he was in command of himself did he join her. She was dressed in her own clothes, slacks and sweater, and for an appalled moment he had the impression that they'd become transparent. He took a deep breath.

Dottie seemed not to notice anything odd in his manner. She was too delighted over the arrival of her breakfast table.

"Oh lovely! I'm dying for a cup of tea."

"Perhaps first you will tell me what happened?" He spoke coldly, for he was under a lot of strain. "Is this some old English tradition that Elluria will have to grow used to. Will sleeping on closet floors become the fashion in society?"

"Don't be silly. Last night I had a bath and went in there looking for a bathrobe, and the door clicked shut behind me. When I tried to open it I found it had locked itself, and I couldn't get any of the others open, either. I thumped and yelled but nobody heard me. I got a bit panicky, but then I realized there was no real problem. When people came in next morning I'd yell and they'd find me. So I settled down to sleep. What's happened to the tea?"

"There isn't any. It's coffee. But you didn't yell, did you?"

"Well, I would have done if I hadn't overslept. How do I get some tea?"

"I'll give orders for it. It's lucky for us all that you snore. Otherwise we wouldn't have found you."

"How dare you say I snore!"

"If you didn't snore you could have been there all day. I was going to send out search parties."

"I see. Bring her back, 'dead or alive.'"

"Just alive," he snapped. "Dead would be no practical use."

"You're all heart," she complained.

"Dottie, don't push me. Right now you're talking to a man who's had a bad fright, and it hasn't left me in the best of moods."

"And you're talking to someone who's spent the night on the floor wearing only her birthday suit."

"There's no need to go into details." he said desperately.

"It hasn't left me feeling that everything's tickety-boo either, especially," she came to her real grievance, "since I can't get a cup of tea. What's the point of being a princess if I can't get a cuppa? I'd be better off in Wenford."

"Where I'm strongly tempted to send you."

"Can't be soon enough for me."

In the seething silence that followed Randolph pressed a bell in the wall, and when Bertha appeared he said, "Her Royal Highness prefers tea with her breakfast. Please see to it immediately."

"Yes, sir. Should that be China tea, Indian tea—"

"Just make sure that it's strong enough to stand the spoon up in," Randolph growled, assailed by memories of breakfast in Wenford.

Bertha curtsied and departed.

Silence.

"Well, you got that right, about the spoon. I'll make an Englishman of you yet," Dottie said, trying to lighten the atmosphere. From the look he threw her she knew she'd failed.

"Where's Mike?" she asked. "I think we should be eating together."

"You can call him on the internal phone. Room 43."

Dottie dialed and was answered at once by an unfamiliar male voice.

"Mike?" she demanded.

"Mr. Kenton is unavailable at the moment. This is his valet."

"His *valet? Mike?* Never mind. Haul him out of the bath. Tell him the love of his life wants to talk to him."

"Mr. Kenton is not in the bath, Your Highness. He has been invited to drive a Ferrari and will be away for the rest of the day."

"I guess I can't compete with a Ferrari," Dottie murmured wryly, hanging up.

"It was only kind to keep him happy while you're

occupied with more weighty matters,'' Randolph said. He'd recovered his poise now, and could only hope that Dottie hadn't guessed the reason for his edginess.

The arrival of strong tea helped the atmosphere. Dottie offered him some, but he declined with a shudder.

''Since you've disposed of my fiancé, I suppose I'm all yours for the day,'' she remarked. ''What's the agenda?''

''Your appearance, clothes, hairstyling etc. After a couple of days of intensive preparation there'll be a press conference.''

''What do I say at that?'' she asked in alarm.

''Absolutely nothing.''

''Pretty pointless press conference, then.''

''Others will do the talking. You will smile and look regal. The point is that you should be seen.''

''Seen and not heard?''

''Exactly.''

''Come to think of it, they'll get a shock when Princess Dottie opens her mouth.''

''Princess Dorothea,'' he corrected her. ''Dottie makes you sound crazy.''

''Well, I am crazy. Always was.''

''You *can't* be Princess Dottie!''

''Fiddle!'' she said firmly. ''I'm Dottie. If they don't like it, they can send me home.''

''We'll address this problem later,'' he growled, adding under his breath, ''among many others.''

Dottie concentrated on her breakfast, refusing to answer this provocation.

''You also need to meet various persons of the court,'' Randolph continued, ''including your future ladies in waiting.''

"Must I have ladies in waiting?" Dottie asked plaintively. "After all, I'll be gone soon. You *are* looking for someone else, aren't you?"

"Diligently," Randolph said. He'd ordered that no stone should be left unturned, in case she carried out her threat to leave. "But as far as the world knows, you've come to stay."

She couldn't resist giving him an impish look. "Now there's an unnerving thought!"

He met her gaze. "Quite. I wonder which of us is more appalled by it."

Her lips twitched. "You probably."

That came too close to home. He turned away from her sharply, pacing the room. And that was how he noticed *Royal Secrets* lying open.

It was the copy he himself had given her and it was entirely reasonable for her to read it, but logic was useless against the revulsion that rose in him at the thought of her learning his most painful secrets in this vulgar way. He had to walk away to the window because he couldn't bear to look at her.

In London she'd charmed him, but that had been another world. Here, where she was taking over his birthright, it was hard for him to regard her without hostility.

He turned, meaning to tell her coldly that her humor was inappropriate, but he met her eyes, fixed on him, and saw the small crinkle of bewilderment in her forehead. She looked smaller, more vulnerable than he remembered, and his anger died. It wasn't her fault.

"Eat your breakfast," he said more gently. "Then Aunt Liz will attend you. She knows all there is to be known about clothes. I suggest you appoint her as your Mistress of Robes, but of course that decision is yours."

The countess was in an ebullient mood, having spent a hugely enjoyable night making plans for Dottie's appearance. She mourned Dottie's lack of height but praised her dainty build.

"We'll have clothes made to measure, but for your appearance this afternoon we will apply to a boutique, fortunately an extremely exclusive establishment. Once we've purchased the garments, they will withdraw them from their range, of course."

"Of course," Dottie murmured. "It'll be interesting to visit some of the shops."

"What are you thinking of? You can't go to a shop."

"Well, it won't come to me, will it?"

Aunt Liz was scandalized. "Of course it will."

Within an hour four young women, trooped in, curtsied and proceeded to display an array of clothes that almost made Dottie weep with ecstasy. She spent two blissful hours trying on, discarding, trying again, changing her mind, going back to the one she'd first thought of. And not once did anyone grow impatient with her.

More young women. Shoes. Underwear. Finally Aunt Liz chose three dresses, "Just to tide you over while your official wardrobe is being made."

"What about paying for them?" Dottie muttered, conscious of everyone looking at her expectantly.

"These matters are dealt with by your Mistress of Robes." The countess paused delicately.

"In that case, Aunt Liz, will you do the honors?"

She had made her first appointment.

A hairstylist appeared and transformed Dottie's

shortish hair into more sophisticated contours. While she was still in rollers she took a bath, and emerged to find her underwear and hose laid out ready.

The dress was simple, cream silk, with a high waistline. The shoes matched it exactly. About her neck she wore a pearl necklace that, Bertha said, had been a gift from the Tsar of Russia to Queen Dorothea I in the eighteenth century. Dottie gulped.

At last she was ready. Everyone curtsied their way out, leaving her to wait for Randolph, who would escort her to the reception. Now she felt good, full of confidence knowing that she looked terrific. She wondered if Randolph would think so.

She wandered out onto her balcony that overlooked the deer park. There was the lake she'd seen last night, blue and beautiful glinting in the afternoon sun. She could pick out the exact spot where the man and woman had walked.

There was a woman standing there now. She didn't move, but stood, looking down into the water, as though sunk in thought, perhaps dreaming of the man, and the intimate moments they'd shared. Suddenly she began to walk purposefully back toward the palace. As she neared the balcony she stopped and raised her head, looking straight at Dottie. It was a direct, challenging gaze, almost angry, and it revealed her face clearly enough for Dottie to recognize her from the magazine photographs.

This was Sophie Bekendorf, Randolph's fiancé, and perhaps the woman he loved.

Dottie sensed that Sophie was looking her over. She was getting used to that, but there was something disagreeable about this woman's manner, and the slightly scornful smile that touched her mouth before she moved on and vanished from sight.

A moment ago she'd felt full of confidence and courage. Now she saw herself for what she was, an impostor, playing a role that was beyond her, and making herself ridiculous. With a sinking heart she went to survey herself again in the mirror. She even looked different, she thought dismally. Everything was wrong.

Randolph found her in this mood. "It's no use," she sighed. "I can't be a princess."

He laid his hands on her shoulders, and spoke gently. "Why ever not?"

"I'm too short."

He frowned. "I beg your pardon?"

"I'm too short. Princesses should be tall and elegant, looking down their noses at everyone, and I'm..." she made a helpless gesture, *"short."*

His lips twitched. He tried to control it but with her wicked little face gazing at him control was impossible.

"What are you laughing at?" she demanded.

"At you, and your scatty way of thinking."

"Well there you are. If people are going to laugh at me I can't be a princess, can I?"

"I won't let anyone laugh at you," he promised.

"Except you."

"Except me."

"But I'm still too short. You couldn't fix me another six inches, could you?"

"Dottie, I would fix you anything you wanted in the world, but I'm afraid that is beyond me. You'll just have to be a short princess. Now stop fretting. I've brought something to show you."

He laid out before her a small painting, in the style of the eighteenth century. It showed a woman of about thirty, at the height of her beauty. On the top of her elaborately arranged hair was a diamond tiara. More diamonds hung from her ears and around her throat was a magnificent diamond necklace, the same one that Dottie was wearing now. They were jewels for a queen, and she wasn't surprised to read, at the foot of the portrait this had been Queen Dorothea I. What did astonish her was the woman's face.

"But...that's me," she gasped.

"It's a family likeness that has carried down through the generations," Randolph agreed. "There is no doubt that you are her descendant, and it will smooth your path as queen." When she didn't answer he frowned slightly. "Dottie? Did you hear me?"

"Yes," she said vaguely, her eyes fixed on the portrait.

Almost in a dream she went to the mirror to look at herself, then back at the picture. It was happening again, the feeling of morphing into somebody else. From a great distance she could hear the voice of Dottie Hebden saying, "I can't do this. Me, a queen? Don't be funny."

Against that she set her own face looking back at her from the portrait. The lips never moved, and yet it spoke to her in a voice she knew, silently telling her that this was where she belonged.

Chapter Five

"Don't try to take it all in," Randolph advised Dottie in the last few seconds before she met the members of her court. "Just smile at everyone."

"I can't smile," she gasped. "My stomach's full of butterflies."

"Trust me."

It was too late for her to say anything more. The heavy gilt doors were being pulled open in front of them, and she was staring along the length of a room that seemed to go on forever. Down the center was a long crimson carpet, leading to a dais, at the top of which was a chair upholstered in crimson plush. A crimson canopy, bearing the royal coat of arms, rose high overhead. The room was lined with faces.

Randolph took her hand in his, holding it up, almost to shoulder height. She wondered if he could feel that she was shaking. Strangely it felt as though he too was shaking. She gave him a quick, disbelieving glance, but he was staring straight ahead. "Lead with the left foot," he murmured. And they were off.

As they walked slowly along the carpet the faces came into focus, so that she could discern bafflement, hostility, but mostly curiosity.

Nearing the dais she murmured to Randolph, "That chair…is it?"

"Yes, it's the throne."

She gulped. "Blimey!"

Randolph's voice was low and fierce. "Dottie, I beg you not to say 'Blimey!'"

"What can I say?" she asked frantically.

"If you must express surprise, 'Goodness me!' would be appropriate." There came a suppressed choke of laughter. *"Dottie!"*

"Well, I can't keep a straight face. I've never said 'Goodness me' in my life."

"Then start saying it now."

During this urgent, whispered conversation they had reached the canopied throne. Dottie turned to confront the people who had moved forward to crowd around the base of the steps, and she felt as well as saw their shock as they gained their first clear view of her face. There was a ripple of astonished recognition. Dorothea.

As before, Randolph made a speech presenting her, and signaled for her to take her place on the throne, while he remained standing. One by one her courtiers advanced and bowed or curtsied while Randolph introduced them. As he'd advised, she didn't try to take it all in, but one name stood out. Sophie Bekendorf.

The tall beauty came forward and looked up at Sophie. It was the same look, defiant, scornful, as she'd seen barely an hour before. And now she realized the full splendor of Sophie's looks. Her skin was pale porcelain, without blemish, her eyes large and dark, her features regular and her chestnut hair glossy. But it was her mouth that would draw everyone's attention, Dottie thought. It was petulant, willful and sensual, a mouth to make a man dream of kissing it, and then dream afterward of how the kiss had felt. How could Randolph not be in love with her? How could he ever love anyone else?

Everyone knew the story and was watching the meeting of the two women with interest, waiting for Sophie to curtsy. But she stayed motionless for so long that a thrilled whisper ran around the crowd. At the very last possible moment Sophie dropped the very smallest possible curtsy, and passed on, her head high.

If Sophie aroused Dottie's dislike, Sophie's brother made the hairs stand up on her spine. Dagbert was handsome, but everything he did seemed naturally insolent, so that the disagreeable effect was stronger than his good looks. He flicked his eyes over Dottie and gave a little dismissive smile. Indignant, she raised her chin and looked over his head.

At last the ceremony was over and she was free to start the walk back down the crimson carpet. When the gilt doors had closed behind her she let out a long breath of relief.

"You did excellently," Randolph said. "You looked right and you had the perfect distant manner."

It was modest enough praise, but she felt a small glow of satisfaction. She guessed Randolph wasn't a man who paid lavish compliments.

''I feel like a puppet whose strings have been suddenly let go. They don't like me.''

''They were all very impressed by you.''

''Not Sophie Bekendorf and her brother. Did you see the way he looked at me? Like I was dirt?''

''Their position is...peculiar,'' Randolph said awkwardly. ''They too have had to adjust to circumstances.''

His tone warned Dottie to inquire no further. As if to keep her off the sensitive subject he hurried on, ''Tonight I thought you and Mike would like to see some of the sights. The city is beautiful by floodlight.''

So Mike wasn't to be kept entirely apart from her, she thought with relief. Perhaps Randolph had accepted that he couldn't win.

Aunt Liz turned her out in style in a silky, flowing creation in pale blue, with a solid silver pendant.

''Enchanting,'' she enthused. ''And this afternoon you were just perfect. I know His Roy— That is, Randolph was thrilled with you.''

''He didn't exactly put it that way,'' Dottie demurred.

''Of course not. You must understand that his standards are of the very highest. For his country, nothing is too good. You won't find him an easy taskmaster. What did he say to you?''

''He said I had the right distant manner.''

''Excellent. He must be really impressed to be so warm in his approval.''

''Yes, but... Oh well, never mind.''

Tonight she could be alone with Mike and tell him of the British ambassador's promise that her reward for holding the fort would be enough money to buy the garage. They could start making plans at once.

Mike too had been newly outfitted and appeared before her in a dinner jacket and black tie. She stared at him, impressed, and he returned the compliment.

"You look great, Dot. Real great. I've got a couple of friends here, who are going to show us the sights." He turned to a handsome young couple in their twenties, who had come in with him. "Harry and Jeanie."

"Count Heinrich and Countess Eugenia Batz," Aunt Liz supplied, while the couple bowed and curtsied.

"You told me Harry and Jeanie," Mike complained to his new friends.

"And so we are," the man said merrily. "Your Royal Highness—"

"Oh no, please," Dottie protested. "I can't stand any more of that. It's such a mouthful every time."

"Isn't it?" Jeanie said gaily. "Protocol is that we just say it once a day, when we first meet you. After that it's ma'am."

"We're all going to have a wonderful night out," Harry said.

So she and Mike weren't to be left alone together, Dottie thought wryly. Randolph had thought of everything.

"I see you're all ready. Splendid." Randolph's voice from the door made them all turn.

Like the other men he was wearing a dinner jacket, and Dottie had to admit that he put them into the shade, not just by being taller, but by a certain air of natural authority, the conviction that wherever he was, he was at home. It had been born and bred into him, and she guessed that he would never lose it now.

His gaze fell on her. She had the feeling that he checked slightly and a faint warmth crept into his eyes.

"Will I do?" she asked, and held her breath for the answer.

"Admirably. You begin to look like a queen."

"Thank you," she said, deflated.

"Tonight you will enjoy yourselves. Harry and Jeanie will show you the best time you've ever had."

"Are you coming too?" Dottie asked.

"No, for once you'll be spared my company. Other duties demand my attention. But I'm leaving you in safe hands."

"Eee Dot, it's gonna be great," Mike enthused.

"You forgot my royal dignity," Dottie teased him. "You should have said, 'Eee *ma'am,* it's gonna be great."

Mike roared with laughter, and in the general mirth they all swept out of the door. Dottie tried not to mind that Randolph wasn't coming too, but it was natural, being used to his undivided attention, to feel a little put out.

In minutes the sleek, black limousine had reached the suburbs of Wolfenberg, the country's capital city. Although not large it was elegant and beautiful, with a Parisian air. The great buildings were constructed from pale gray stone and so cleverly built that the heavy material seemed to take wing. It was growing dark and the floodlights were already on.

"There's the parliament building," Jeanie pointed out, "the town hall, the cathedral and there's the great fountain that was built to commemorate the battle of..."

For Dottie these things were interesting, but she

knew that Mike would be going glassy-eyed with boredom. She asked him about his day and he needed no encouragement to talk about the Ferrari. Since Harry too was a car fanatic the conversation became mechanical, and they soon abandoned sightseeing.

"There's a little place just ahead that I think you'd like," Harry said and soon the car swung into a pretty piazza. A short flight of steps led to a picturesque café with tables outside.

The place specialized in ice cream, and since Dottie was an ice-cream addict she felt she was in heaven. It was a warm evening. In the piazza just below them were trees hung with colored lights, beneath which couples strolled.

"This is the center of Wolfenberg," Jeanie explained as Dottie tucked into a huge confection of chocolate, coffee and vanilla ice cream, studded with nuts and doused in cream. "People congregate here before and after the theater, and sooner or later everyone comes past."

As if to prove her right Dagbert appeared from under the trees, and hailed them. "My friends! How nice to see you!"

He was full of bonhomie, demanding an introduction to Mike, bowing very correctly to Dottie. She greeted him coolly, remembering his air of dismissive contempt earlier that day, but tonight Dagbert was on his best behavior. He began to tell Dottie about the city, especially the cathedral, "where your coronation will be held." She began to wonder if she'd misjudged him.

"It's getting a little chilly," Harry said at last. "Perhaps we should find some entertainment indoors?" He smiled at Dottie. "We also have excellent nightclubs. Robin Anthony, for instance, is singing at The Birdcage."

"Robin Anthony?" Dottie exclaimed in delight. "I've been madly in love with him for years."

"You never told me," Mike observed mildly.

"Yes I did. You took me to one of his concerts for my seventeenth birthday, and snored all the way through."

"Oh yeah, I remember now."

"But could we still get in?" she asked anxiously. "His concerts were always sold out."

"They won't be sold out for you," Dagbert observed.

"Oh yes, I forgot. Maybe, I'm going to enjoy this."

Dottie wasn't sure what he told the manager but they were ushered to a table at the front, and she was treated with a discreet deference that she had to admit was pleasant.

"The trouble is," she confided to Mike in an undervoice, "that after one day I'm already becoming spoiled. I warn you, when we get home I'll expect it."

"Don't you worry Dot. I'll bring you a cuppa in bed every morning."

Dottie squeezed his arm, overwhelmed by tenderness and affection for him. How could she have imagined anything would be better than being married to Mike?

Robin Anthony was a disappointment, past his best, putting on weight and living on his reputation.

"Oh dear!" Dottie sighed as he bowed his way off. "Goodbye my teenage dreams."

"May I have the honor of dancing with my future queen?" Dagbert asked as the band struck up.

"I never learned posh dancing," Dottie protested.

"It's only a waltz. I'll teach you."

She let him lead her onto the floor. As he'd promised she found the steps easy, and was beginning to get the hang of waltzing, even to enjoy it.

"Don't keep looking down at your feet," Dagbert urged her. "Have confidence. Head up."

She raised her chin and her feet seemed to find their way of their own accord. The glittering lights of the club spun around her, tables, faces. Two faces that she knew.

"Steady!" Dagbert said. "You nearly tripped."

"I—just missed my footing," she stammered.

Another turn of the dance and the little scene passed before her eyes again. A far table, discreetly near the wall, a man and a woman, holding hands, leaning forward so that their heads were almost touching, talking intimately. Randolph and Sophie.

"I'd like to sit down now," she said.

"But I thought you were enjoy—"

"Now," she said sharply. All her original distaste for him was rushing back. This might have been a coincidence, but she would have bet her kingdom on Dagbert having known where his sister would be tonight.

He'd counted on being the king's brother-in-law, and probably milking that for all it was worth. This was a warning to her that he wanted the old order restored, and the battle wasn't over.

But then, she too wanted the old order restored, so there was nothing to mind about. And if Randolph's "other duties" included a romantic dinner with his fiancée, that was just fine by her.

Just the same, she suggested that they all return to the palace, and since her word was law, everyone agreed.

Over her breakfast the next morning, Bertha informed her that Randolph would wait on her to discuss the day.

"You mean he'll come and tell me what I've got to do?" Dottie asked wryly.

"Well, His Roy— I mean, Randolph—"

"Why did you stop yourself?"

"He isn't a 'Royal Highness' anymore," Bertha confided.

"What is he?"

"Nothing. Nobody. It's hard to know how to treat him. We all keep curtsying out of habit, but he gets very cross and tells us not to."

How much self-discipline would that take? Dottie wondered. Perhaps a royal upbringing helped you to go through life smiling when you had to, behaving beautifully when your heart was breaking and concealing your thoughts and feelings. She tried to imagine herself acting so coolly, and retired, defeated.

Emerging from her bath she found Aunt Liz ready with a riding habit, "for your first lesson."

"Am I going to learn to ride?"

"Those are my instructions."

So Randolph gave orders over her head and relayed them to her via a third person. Dottie reckoned you didn't have to be a queen to be annoyed at that. But it was hard to stay cross when the snugly fitting habit showed off her trim figure and neat behind. She was admiring herself in the mirror when Randolph's voice said, "You are one of those rare women who can wear tight pants."

"I can, can't I?" she said gleefully. This was no time for false modesty.

His own riding pants were also snug-fitting, confirming what she'd only suspected before, that his hips were narrow, and his stomach flat. His long legs, the thighs heavy with muscles, might have been created for such a garb. He was standing in his shirtsleeves, leaning against the wall, smiling like a man without a care in the world. But who could tell? she thought, remembering Bertha's words.

"Why riding?" she asked.

"Riding is a social grace, like dancing. When a foreign head of state visits you, you dance with him, and ride with him."

"Then I'll need dancing lessons as well."

"Yes, I heard about last night. I gather you managed very well."

"Didn't you see me fumbling around? You were there with Sophie."

"Yes, I was there with Sophie. Is there any reason why I should not have been?"

His eyes had lost their warmth and become as bleak and chilly as a moorland fog. For a moment she had a glimpse of a hostility that was all the more alarming for being usually hidden.

He seemed to realize that he'd given himself away for he recovered at once, and smiled. "Forgive me. I'm just not used to having my actions questioned."

"But I didn't question your actions," she said indignantly. "I merely mentioned having noticed you. There was no need to get fired up."

"True. I'm a little oversensitive. I apologize if I offended you."

The face was friendly but the tone was formal, and it impelled her to say, "Don't talk like that."

"Like what?"

"As though I was the queen."

"But you are the queen," he said quietly, "and I never can forget it."

"Then the sooner I'm gone the better. I couldn't live like this, people treating me as one person when I feel like someone else inside."

"Not a person, a monarch."

"Well a monarch's still a person."

"No, a symbol," he said quickly. "And if behind that symbol a person lurks, then she—or he—must keep that a secret, and never allow it to influence their behavior. The only thing that matters is what's good for your country. For that good, you must learn to be ruthless, to yourself first of all. Sometimes also to others, but mostly..." his voice grew heavy, "mostly to yourself."

But in a moment he became cheerful again. "But that's enough dull stuff for today. Just now I want you to enjoy your new life."

"So that I become so seduced by the goodies that I can't bear to give them up?" she said cheekily.

"Remind me never to underestimate you," he growled. "Enough. Your instructor is waiting at the stable. Let's go."

Dottie's nerves about riding vanished with the first lesson. Helmut, an elderly army sergeant who'd taught Randolph to ride, had a fierce aspect but a gentle manner. He'd found a docile little mare called Gretel for her. She was a pale honey color, with a

Chapter Six

Within hours the press conference had beamed around the world. Television channels showed it again and again, always focusing on the wonderful moment when Dottie had lifted little Elsa in her arms.

The Ellurian newspapers hailed her as Our Laughing Princess. Some played up the family resemblance. Others claimed she'd already showed how she would be "A true mother to her people."

"On the basis of one incident?" Dottie demanded over breakfast two days later.

"But it was great, Dot," Mike said. He'd dropped in to tell her he'd be out sailing all day. "Just fancy, your grandpa being right all along!"

"Did he bend your ear with those stories, too?"

"Only the once. He took me to the pub. We got real plastered, and he came out with all this stuff about Duke Egghead."

''Egbert. What did he say about him?''

''Well that's it, after I'd sobered up I couldn't remember, and I never have. When I get tiddly again it starts coming back to me, but it goes again.''

Those who'd feared, or hoped, that Dottie's unorthodox ways might bring her down were confounded. She was a darling. That was official. Her oddities were no more than charming eccentricity, only to be expected in one who'd been reared ''with wider horizons than royalty normally enjoys.''

Even Randolph raised a smile at that. He was delighted at the way people were determined to see the best in her, even though the facts behind the headlines sometimes made him tear his hair.

He hadn't, for instance, been amused when Dottie vanished again, and turned up in the kitchen, chatting happily with the cooks and eating ice cream ''like a greedy child,'' as he caustically put it.

''Well, I tucked in because I was sure you were going to arrive any minute and spoil the party,'' Dottie told him, adding gloomily, ''And you did.''

She didn't mention the fun she'd had reducing Fritz, the head chef, to jelly. But Fritz invented a new ice cream which became known as The Dottie Special, despite horrified attempts by the palace old guard to quell the name.

Dottie fell on it with delight, even ordering it for breakfast one morning, and sending down a note with the empty dishes saying. *Dear Fritz, terrific as always. How about doing one with peaches? Ever yours, HRH, Dottie.*

Somehow the story got into the papers and vastly increased her popularity, which might, or might not, have been the intention of the person who leaked it.

Messages of congratulations began to flood in from governments and royal houses, including one from Prince Harold of Korburg, that made Randolph snort with disgust.

He had an air of tension these days, the reason for which everybody guessed, although it was spoken only in whispers. Dottie's acceptance as the true heir had finally broken the patience of the Bekendorf family. Sophie's father had stormed in to see Randolph and finally broken the engagement. The Bekendorfs did not marry nobodies.

Hearing the story, Dottie winced, imagining what that cruel barb must have done to a man of Randolph's pride.

"Don't believe the lurid tales," Aunt Liz advised. "Randolph's valet is married to my maid, and I can tell you that Randolph did *not* knock the man to the floor, nor did he make a noble speech about true love conquering all, which is the other version doing the rounds. He merely observed that he had already freed Sophie from all obligation to him, and asked Bekendorf to leave."

"Poor Randolph," Dottie murmured. "How terrible he must feel."

Aunt Liz shrugged. "I suppose he must, but he'll never tell anybody."

Dottie nodded, thinking of the magical evening they'd spent together, when she'd seen only what he wanted her to see, the smiling charm, the pleasure in a shared joke. And all the time...

She tried to remember his eyes, and could recall only their warmth. Even his remoteness had been hidden that night, while he'd encouraged her to open her mind as she'd done to nobody else. And she felt again the little flame of resentment against him.

The days began to merge into each other, and slip away, each one too packed with activity for Dottie to think. When she wasn't being fitted for new clothes and wearing the triumphant results at receptions, she was discovering Elluria on horseback. Now it was Randolph who escorted her through the countryside, full of spring blossoms. He often smiled at her eager pleasure in her surroundings.

"Anyone would think you'd never seen the countryside before," he said once.

"In a way that's true. I've always lived in London. I never knew anything as beautiful as this."

They had dismounted to let their horses drink from a stream that ran through a small wood. When the beasts were satisfied, Dottie and Randolph tied them to a tree and wandered away by the water. Ahead of them the sunlight slanted between the branches, and the light seemed to mingle with the sound of birdsong and the soft crunch of their feet against the earth. At moments like this she wished it would never end. There was peace here, something she dimly recognized that she had never found before.

Randolph walked beside her in silence, handsome and maddeningly unreadable. Dottie longed to say something to comfort his sadness, but she guessed he would hate for her to introduce the subject, and she couldn't risk it. Lacking any other way to reach out to him, she showed her sympathy by a careful gentleness. At last he said, wryly humorous, "Dottie, please don't treat me with kid gloves. I promise you it isn't necessary."

"I can't help it. I heard what happened."

"It was bound to happen. Bekendorf couldn't let the situation continue. No father could."

"But doesn't Sophie get a say?"

He looked across the water. "Sophie has been more loyal to me than I deserve. She would have abandoned everything to marry me, even as a commoner. I can't accept her sacrifice, although I honor her for her generosity."

"But do you lo—"

"Please can we discuss it no further? The matter is ended."

"If you can end it just like that, then..." She stopped at the look in his eyes.

"Yes," he said dangerously, "Go on. Am I in for some sentimental psychobabble about not having loved her? The only true feelings are the ones that are paraded to the world? Because I don't bare my soul on *Oprah,* I *have* no soul? Isn't that how it goes?"

She didn't answer, only stood looking at him. He sighed and calmed down.

"I'm sorry. I shouldn't have lost my temper with you."

"Probably did you good," she said. "I can't see you blurting it out on *Oprah* either, but keeping it all in isn't good for you. All right, that's psychobabble, but sometimes even psychobabble gets it right. You're too controlled."

"Control was instilled in me as a child. It's too late for me to abandon it now."

"But don't you ever want to be simply happy?"

His answer was an eloquent shrug, and suddenly, as if a window had been opened, she saw into his mind. "You don't think happiness matters, do you?"

"Not for me," he said in a matter-of-fact tone that had no trace of self-pity.

"What does matter to you?"

"My duty to the people of this country, in one way, if not another."

"You mean teaching me to take your place?"

"Of course."

"But doesn't that hurt terribly?"

"It doesn't matter," he shouted. "Why can't you understand that? Whether it hurts me or not is unimportant. Let me tell you—" he checked and took a deep breath.

"Tell me what?"

"That life is a great deal easier this way. There's nothing worse than constantly fretting over your own feelings. There's no happiness in that either. But if you do what has to be done, there can be a little satisfaction."

Something was aching inside her, almost too much for her to speak. "And that's what you're going to live for?" she asked at last. "A little satisfaction from doing your duty."

"It's all that's left for me, Dottie."

"But you can't say that," she cried. "It's giving up on life."

"I shall live a life—"

"No you won't, except on the surface. Inwardly you'll have crawled away into a cave where you think nobody can find you. You say that being hurt doesn't matter, but actually you plan to protect yourself by not having any feelings that *can* be hurt. It looks brave and noble but actually it's cowardly."

"Thank you," he snapped. "If you've finished..."

"I haven't. There's something else."

"Get it over with."

"All right," she said breathlessly, and kissed him.

She did it quickly before she lost her nerve, but she was driven by a need so strong that it created a kind of courage. The last time her lips had lain against his had been in the park on her final day in England. The memory had been with her every moment since, and now there was something she had to know. Seeking the answer, she pressed her mouth more urgently against his, and felt his tremor, his indecision. He wanted to draw back but couldn't make himself do it. She sensed that much. But what else was there?

His hands were on her shoulders, neither pushing her away nor drawing her close. In a troubled voice he murmured, "Dottie..."

"I'm not going to let you hide in that cave."

She had a glimpse of his face, harsh and cynical as he said, "Perhaps that isn't your decision."

"I'm the crown princess, I'm making it my decision."

She silenced him before he could answer, kissing him again with purpose and urgency. Her life hadn't taught her to be a skilled lover, but she had something better than skill, a need to communicate with him through her flesh, and a feeling in her heart that she wouldn't acknowledge, but which drove her none the less.

She could feel him trembling with the struggle going on inside, and she sensed the exact moment when he stopped struggling. He'd been holding himself taut in defense against her, but suddenly the tension went out of him and his body seemed to relax against her. Then his arms went around her and he had taken charge, full of anger and resentment at how she'd broken through his guard, but unable to prevent it.

"You're playing a dangerous game, Dottie," he growled.

"Who's playing games?" she whispered against his mouth. "Kiss me."

She barely got the last word out before he smothered her mouth again, kissing her with a fierce skill that showed her she was just an amateur. But she was learning fast. Sliding her hands along his arms, feeling the swell of muscles, it was as though she'd never touched a man before. Nor had she. Only boys, as unskilled as herself, callow lads who'd deferred to "Steamroller Dottie." But this man had deferred to nobody until she came along, and now he was in no mood to defer to her. She'd unleashed something she couldn't control, and it was the most thrilling event of her life.

Her heart was hammering. Briefly, it was alarming how everything was slipping out of focus, but then she didn't care anymore. Nothing mattered beyond this moment, her old life, her new life, Mike...

Mike!

She pulled back, gasping as the world returned abruptly. "Oh no, I can't...please let me go."

He did so, staring at her with a brow of thunder. Even so, he was more in command than she.

"I shouldn't have done that," she said in horror. "Why didn't you stop me?"

"Her Royal Highness's word is law," Randolph said ironically.

"Is that the only reason why you kissed me back? To humor me?"

"Is that why you think I did?"

"Don't confuse me with questions. Oh, I'm terrible. How could I do that to poor Mike?"

Randolph made a sound of disgust. "Do you realize that's how you always talk about him? To you he's always *poor* Mike. If a woman's really in love with a man she doesn't talk about him like that."

"That's not true," she flashed. "I've always been in love with Mike."

"Perhaps that's why you aren't anymore," he suggested, his eyes full of the things she was trying to pretend weren't true.

"You know nothing about it."

"I know how you kissed me just now. I know that it was *your* kiss. What more do I need to know?"

"That's right, jeer at me."

"I'm not jeering, merely pointing out that all this maidenly reticence is a little out of place."

"Because I came on to you, right? Well, I shouldn't have done, and I wish I hadn't. I'd forgotten what you're really like."

"And what am I really like?"

"Everything's planned, isn't it? Draw people in so that you can use them, and then fend them off when they try to be nice to you. Oh boy, am I glad I'm going home soon!"

"Dottie, listen—"

"No, I'm going back. Don't come with me."

"I have to."

Suddenly inspired she flashed, "Then you can follow me 'at a respectful distance.' There! Is that royal enough for you?"

She fled back to her horse, so furiously upset that she actually managed to mount without assistance, which she usually couldn't do. By the time Randolph reached his own horse she was far ahead, galloping madly.

All over Elluria the mail deliveries were being watched with feverish excitement. A grand ball would put the seal on the new queen's acceptance, and not to be invited meant social death. As the last of the invitations arrived there were sighs of relief and groans of despair.

The chandeliers in the great ballroom were taken down and each tiny facet washed separately. The finest crystal was retrieved from cupboards. The palace gardeners worked overtime tending hothouse blooms to adorn the public rooms.

Dottie's dress was a masterpiece of blue satin, heavily embroidered and studded with jewels. On her head she would wear a diamond tiara that had been in the family for three hundred years. A matching diamond necklace and bracelet completed her adornment.

"You look gorgeous, Dot," Mike breathed when he looked in on a fitting. Aunt Liz had stepped out for a moment and they were alone.

She wondered fleetingly how she would look to Randolph. Would he think her beautiful? He'd been away for the past couple of days, and she didn't know when he'd return. That was good, she told herself. The thought of their last meeting still made her go hot and cold with shame.

"Dot? Are you there?"

"Sorry," she said hastily, returning to the present. "How are you managing, darling? I gather they're fixing you up with white tie and tails!"

He made a face in which disgust and unease were

mingled, and she burst out laughing. Then she kissed him more tenderly than usual. She was feeling guilty about Mike these days.

"And I'm having dancing lessons," he said. "I told them I didn't need that. A waltz is easy—one, two, three, one, two, three. What else do you need?"

"I said the same," Dottie replied, carefully removing the magnificent jewelry. "But I have to learn all the other stuff, too. Fancy doing the quickstep and wondering if your tiara's falling off.

"Undo me," she begged. He pulled down the zip at the back, and steadied her as she stepped out of the dress. Still in her slip, she draped the lovely dress over the back of a chair then turned to him with mischief in her eyes. "One, two, three?" she said.

"You're on. Can I have the first waltz, madam?"

But she shook her head in mock horror. "Oh no, you have to wait for me to invite you. If I deign to honor you, a footman will approach and ask if you would like 'the honor of dancing with Her Royal Highness.'"

"Suppose I say no?"

"Then I'll lock you up for an insult to my royal person."

"You're a right idiot, you know that, Dot?"

"You only just found that out?"

They laughed together and began hopping around the room like the pair of kids they had once been.

Mike's brow became furrowed, as it always did when he tried to think. "Don't feel you have to invite me to this big 'do,'" he said. One, two, three. "I wouldn't be offended if you thought I'd be out of place."

"You're not getting out of it that easily," she said,

interpreting this generous offer without difficulty. "I'll need moral support." One, two, three.

"But Dot..."

"Be there."

"Yes, Dot. Anything you say Dot."

"And don't say it like that, as though I'm always giving you orders."

"No, Dot. Anything you say Dot."

She thumped his arm. He began to chuckle and she joined in, overwhelmed by tender affection for him. He was her Mike, as comfortable as an old slipper, and right now that seemed preferable to the turbulent sensations and feelings that awaited her if she wasn't careful. At last they stopped dancing and clung together, while peals of mirth echoed up to the elegant painted ceiling.

Their laughter reached Randolph, who was approaching along the corridor and through the outer room. The sound entranced him, catching at his heart and making him press forward to find the source without considering what it might be. The door to her bedroom was ajar and he'd pushed it open and walked in before he had time to think. That was how he saw Dottie, dressed in her slip, hugging Mike to her, her head thrown back as she laughed affectionately up into his face.

"Good afternoon," Randolph said calmly.

Dottie released herself from Mike's arms, but didn't seem discomposed at being found like this. If anything, she eyed Randolph with dislike, which puzzled Mike.

"I believe Captain Gorshin and some of his friends were hoping you would join them about now," Randolph informed him.

"Right. Fine. 'Bye Dot."

When they were alone Randolph eyed her coldly. "May I suggest that you put some clothes on?" he said bleakly. "May I further suggest that in future you pay a little more attention to the proprieties? Fooling around with young men in your underwear is not the behavior this country expects of its queen."

He spoke more harshly than he'd intended. The intimate sight he'd stumbled on had struck him like a blow in the chest. He called formality to his aid, and for once it failed him.

"And may I remind you that these are my private apartments and you should have knocked before coming in?" Dottie said defiantly. "May I further remind you that in these rooms *I* decide what's proper and what isn't?"

"Congratulations, Dottie," he said ironically. "You're beginning to acquire the tone of lofty command. It's a pity you have such a poor idea of when to use it."

"Are you telling me how to behave?"

"On the evidence of my eyes I think somebody needs to."

"Oh stop being so stuffy. Mike's seen me in less than this—"

"I don't want the details."

"—when I stayed with his family once, and we all had to fight over the bathroom." She met his eyes innocently. "Everyone saw everyone in everything...or rather in nothing. Or anyway, not much." Seeing no yielding in his face she said coaxingly, "Can't you see the funny side?"

"I suppose I might have expected that from you,"

he said bitterly. "The funny side. Always the funny side. You're incurably frivolous."

"Rubbish. I can be serious when the situation is serious. But this one isn't."

"You're the queen. If you let a man see you wearing only a slip and—" he stopped, feeling his breath coming unevenly.

Dottie looked down at herself, following his gaze. "Yes, I'm not wearing a bra," she said. She couldn't resist adding, "Have you only just noticed?"

He'd been trying not to. The top of her slip was lacy and full of little holes, giving tantalizing glimpses of her otherwise bare breasts. They were as firm and uptilted as he recalled from that first morning when he'd been granted a brief, forbidden glimpse of her lovely nakedness. His brow was damp.

"Are you so shameless that you don't cover yourself?" he demanded coldly.

Dottie herself couldn't have explained what had gotten into her to make her goad him like this, but the little devil that was urging her on gave another prod with his trident.

"Why should I? It's only you."

"Meaning that I'm some kind of eunuch?" he demanded dangerously.

"I was thinking more of a father figure. And what's a eunuch?"

"A eunuch would be a man who could see a woman dressed as you are and feel no response," he snapped. "A eunuch would observe you half-naked *and see the funny side.*"

"But you don't?"

A pit yawned at his feet. Just in time he saw it and swerved.

"I cannot be amused," he said bitingly, "when a woman to whom I must swear allegiance as my queen behaves in a way unsuitable to her station."

The effect of these words on Dottie was so swift and dramatic that it took Randolph aback. He couldn't know that any reference to his lowered position cut her to the heart. He only knew that the fun drained out of her face, leaving only a sad dignity behind.

"Perhaps you're right," she said, pulling on a robe and turning away from him.

"Dottie, I was only—"

"It's a rotten situation for you. I should have remembered."

"Let's not discuss that."

"No, we don't need to discuss anything. I'll go and get dressed now."

She hurried away, leaving Randolph displeased with himself. He'd acted correctly and it had been a disaster. She was no longer joyous, therefore no longer Dottie.

And that was all wrong.

The rules stated that royalty arrived last and departed first. So on the night of the great ball Dottie stood, with Randolph, behind the huge mirrored double doors that led into the ballroom, knowing that on the other side were gathered two thousand people.

She would have liked to grasp his hand, but although he was beside her she couldn't make herself do it. Everything was wrong between them now.

The moment came. From behind the doors she could hear the orchestra play the national anthem. The doors opened on the glittering scene and they stepped forward.

At once she was engulfed in a wave of applause. Everywhere people were smiling at her. She knew a stab of pleasure, but hard on its heels came indignation. Why didn't they hate her for displacing the man whose life was dedicated to their service? Why didn't they spare a thought for his suffering? Burning with pity for him, she failed to notice her progress until she found herself at the foot of the stairs leading to her dais.

Randolph led her to the top, inclined his head and withdrew. The Master of Ceremonies caught her eye. She nodded, he signaled to the orchestra conductor, her partner presented himself and the ball began.

Deep in the crowd, Mike had watched Dottie's arrival with fond admiration, glad to see that she didn't seem to need his help. Then a footman approached him, but the words weren't the ones he'd expected. "Would you like the honor of dancing with the Countess Sophie Bekendorf?"

Mike looked around wildly at some of his officer friends, but they slapped him on the back and urged him on. Sophie was magnificent in dark red velvet, her shoulders bare but for the famous Bekendorf rubies. Feeling like a lamb being led to slaughter Mike followed the footman toward her, not in the least comforted by her brilliant smile.

But Sophie was charming. She greeted him warmly and was even understanding about his dancing. After a couple of turns around the floor she said sympathetically, "Why don't we sit this one out? I'm a little thirsty."

Mike found himself in a small conservatory just off the ballroom, a drink in his hand, and Sophie's ardent eyes turned on him.

"I really only drink beer," he protested.

"But this wine is practically our national drink," she said, sounding hurt.

So he tried it, and had to admit that it wasn't bad after all.

"Everyone wants to talk to you," Sophie said admiringly, "because nobody knows our new queen as well as you. We're all so glad to have her. She's refreshingly natural."

"Aye, speaks her mind, does Dot," Mike confirmed.

"So I've observed. Tell me, did her royal birth really come as a surprise to her?"

"Oh yes. She had no idea. Mind you, her grandpa always knew. Used to say all sorts when he'd had a few."

Sophie gave a tinkling laugh and Mike began to feel that perhaps he was a heck of a fellow after all. He drained the second glass and a third appeared as if by magic. Or perhaps it was the fourth.

"But I don't suppose he knew very much," she said.

"Well, he had some very strange stories. Nobody believed a word of them, mind." Mike held out his glass to Dagbert, wondering why he'd ever been worried. A glow of content was settling over him.

Deep in the ballroom Dottie was beginning to feel relieved. So far she'd managed without mishap. Every foreign ambassador had to be honored with a dance in strict order of importance. Somewhere near the lower end of the list was Count Graff, the ambassador from Korburg, who danced correctly, spoke like a robot and barely bothered to conceal the fact that he was looking her over with mingled interest and contempt.

Sometimes she caught sight of Randolph, splendid in dress uniform. He too was doing duty dances, although her quick eyes never saw him in Sophie's arms. Why? she wondered. Had they made a pact to avoid each other in this public place? Or was Randolph simply too heartbroken to be near her?

Then she realized that he never looked at her. She'd dared to be pleased with her own appearance. She knew that she really looked like a princess. And for all the notice he took she might as well not have bothered.

At last her duty dances were done, and she could sit on the plush chair on her dais, and wiggle her toes. Randolph would approach her now, but he seemed deep in conversation with a general, so Dottie set her chin and summoned a footman.

"Inform my cousin that I would like to speak to him," she said, sounding more imperious than she felt because she felt uneasy behaving like this.

After a moment Randolph approached her and bowed correctly. His air was polite but formal. He bowed again when she indicated the chair beside her, and took it.

"Is there some way I can be of use to you?" he asked.

"You can tell me how I've offended you."

"Your Royal Highness has not offended me."

"Oh stop that!" she said, letting her temper flare a little. "Why haven't you asked me to dance?"

"Because it's not my place. I've already explained that it's for you—"

"But surely that doesn't apply to you?"

"I'm afraid it does."

"Then I'm asking you to dance with me."

He rose and extended his arm. "As Your Royal Highness commands."

She was about to speak to him crossly again but she noticed how sad his face was, and it silenced her. They danced together correctly for a few minutes, and Dottie became more depressed every minute. When had they ever been correct? Perhaps his misery over Sophie was more than he could conceal. Whatever the cause, he seemed to have become almost a stranger.

He saw her looking at him and smiled self-consciously. "I trust you're enjoying your first ball?" he said.

"Thank you," she said. "I'm enjoying it extremely." She thought that sounded about right.

Randolph heard the elegant phrasing and his heart sank. For some reason tonight he found himself remembering their first evening in London, when she'd laughed and talked outrageously. At first he'd been shocked, but shock had passed as he became charmed by her springlike freshness. And all the while he'd been deceiving her, and he knew that she'd never quite forgiven him.

Now a change had come over her. She was beginning to learn her role, to dress correctly and speak elegantly. But, inch by inch, she was ceasing to be Dottie, and he didn't like it.

He reminded himself that to her this was just a game, that she was looking forward to calling a halt and returning home to marry Mike, the man to whom her heart clung with a stubbornness that drove him wild. He thought of the secret action he'd taken to ensure that her dream would never come true. He was deceiving her again, and his guilt tormented him.

For a moment her attention was distracted, and he followed her gaze to where Sophie was floating by in the arms of the Korburg ambassador, the third time she'd danced with him.

Oh, no! he thought in dismay. *Please Sophie, not that!*

He didn't blame her. He knew the family pressure she was under to find a royal husband, and Harold was now the most eligible. But he felt sick at the thought that she might ally herself with a man he despised. Then he realized that Dottie was watching his face, and he hastily smiled.

The dance was coming to an end. He led her back to her dais, bowed and excused himself. Suddenly feeling very lonely, Dottie looked around for Mike, but there was no sign of him. What she did see was Randolph approaching Sophie and firmly cutting out the Korburg ambassador. She watched miserably as they circled the floor, until Aunt Liz touched her arm and indicated somebody that she really ought to honor with her attention.

For a while Randolph and Sophie waltzed in silence. But at last he could contain himself no longer and said in a soft, urgent voice, ''Don't do it, Sophie. For pity's sake, don't do it.''

''Are you the man who should say that to me?'' she asked softly. ''What else should I do? Wear the willow for you?''

''No, not that, but how could we marry when I have nothing to offer? There was no choice for either of us. Your father made me see that.''

"I understand. Forgive me for what I said, beloved. You're a good man. I know your heart too is broken."

A frisson of unease went through him. Perhaps she sensed it, for she gave a beautifully modulated sob.

"Sophie, please," he murmured. "Don't cry here."

Swiftly he danced her out onto the terrace. She was still weeping, and he felt vaguely embarrassed, and then ashamed of his embarrassment. Once he'd thought her cool, composed, a good friend but no more. Her apparent desolation at his loss made him awkwardly conscious that his own feelings had always been weaker.

"Sophie, my dear," he said as they slowed to a halt, "what do you want me to do?"

"I know you can't change anything," she sobbed. "I accept it, but you mustn't blame me for what I do."

"How could I ever blame you? But it hurts me to think of you as that man's wife."

"And yet you yourself will soon be married, won't you?"

"Hush," he placed his fingertips gently over her mouth. "Don't speak of that."

"No, there's nothing more to say, for either of us. Kiss me goodbye."

Saddened by her grief, and what he felt to be his own inadequate response, he drew her close and laid his lips tenderly on hers. It was the kiss of a generous friend, but from a short distance it could have had the appearance of a lovers' embrace.

At least, that was how it seemed to Dottie, standing at a window, looking out with bleak eyes.

Chapter Seven

Mike appeared in her room at noon next day, hung-over and apologetic.

"Don't know what was in that stuff I drank," he said. "Maybe I should have stuck to beer." He rubbed his head.

"What made you change the habits of a lifetime?" Dottie asked. She too wasn't feeling at her best today.

"I didn't want to offend Countess Bekendorf. Mind you, she wasn't so bad."

"What on earth did you find to talk about?"

"It was some of the stuff your grandpa told me, about your royal ancestors."

"But you told me you couldn't remember that."

"I can't when I'm sober, but last night I wasn't sober."

"So what was it?"

Mike looked rueful. "Sorry Dot, I'm sober again now."

"Oh well," Dottie sighed, "she was bound to try to find out if I'm an impostor. So now she knows that I'm the real thing. Not that it matters. They'll find someone else soon, and then you and I can go home and get married."

She was eager for their departure. There was something about this place that made her behave unlike herself. It wasn't Dottie who'd insisted on kissing Randolph. Nor was it Dottie who'd teased him with her half-clad body, determined to get a response from him and bitterly satisfied when she received one. Dottie would never behave like that because she loved Mike, and it was love that mattered, not lust.

Lust. She considered it, trying to see it in relation to herself. All right, she admitted at last. She fancied Randolph. Fancied him like mad, if the truth be told. But that wasn't real life.

She didn't see him for a couple of days. He'd left in the early hours after the ball and gone to an estate he had nearby. She left a message for him, and he came to her as soon as he returned.

"You should have found another heir by now," she said quietly.

"But I haven't. There's only you."

"But I have to go back to England."

"Are you going to abandon us?" Randolph demanded fiercely. "You have a short memory if you can forget how the people of this country have welcomed you. You know what our fate will be if you desert us."

"They can put you back on the throne," she said

desperately. "It should be you by rights. I'm all wrong. You've said so often enough, and it's true."

"Yes, it is, but it doesn't matter. I'm illegitimate and therefore barred from the throne."

"Well, they can have a what d'you call it? Referee—"

"Referendum."

"Referendum. People can vote for you to be king and then you can marry Sophie and everything will be all right." She hadn't meant to add that last bit.

"If I tried to claim the throne, even with the consent of parliament and the people, Harold would use that as an excuse to start a war. And if I stand back and let him become king, he'll plunder the country and crush its people. The only person who can stop that is you."

"And where does Mike come in your grand scheme of things?"

"He doesn't. You can't marry him. Surely you've realized that?"

"You mean I should just dump him? Oh, lovely. Sorry Mike, it's been nice knowing you but something better has turned up. A nice opinion of me you have! Remember how it felt to lose Sophie?"

The bleak, guarded look that she dreaded appeared in Randolph's eyes. "Why don't we go and talk to Mike?" he asked smoothly. "He's surely entitled to express an opinion."

"I see your game. You'll give him the fancy speech you've just given me, and then you think he'll make the grand sacrifice."

"I admit I don't associate him with grand sacrifices. He impresses me as a very down-to-earth young man, doing everything for prosaic reasons."

"Right! And he'll tell you to jump in the lake."

"I'm trembling."

"And then *I'll* tell you to jump in the lake, and since I'm the crown princess you'll have to do it."

"At Her Royal Highness's command I'll jump in any lake you care to name. Would you like me to wear a lead weight about my neck?"

"Don't be funny with me, buster!"

As they talked Randolph had contrived to urge her out of the door that led to one of the hidden corridors. Dottie followed him, furiously angry. At last she found herself on a little landing, outside a nondescript door. Randolph took a key and unlocked it, ushering her forward. She strode into the room, ready to confront Mike, but the sight that met her eyes drove everything else out of her mind.

Stretched out on the grandiose bed, her eyes closed in pleasure, lay a naked young woman. The rest of her face was obscured by the back of Mike's head. He was also naked, and far too occupied with what he was doing to realize that his fiancée had entered the room. Only drastic action was going to get through to him, so Dottie took it, raising her hand high above her head and bringing it down hard on his vigorously working rump.

His yell of surprise and outrage hit the ceiling. Wriggling away to escape, he contrived to fall right off the bed, landing in an undignified heap at her feet, and revealing the identity of his companion, who screamed as she saw Dottie's doom-laden face.

"You've got a nerve, Bren," Dottie told her. "But I'll come to you later, when I've thumped *him* to kingdom come and back."

"Now, Dot," Mike said from the floor where he

was haplessly trying to cover himself and squirm away from her at the same time. "Don't lose your sense of proportion."

"I don't have one," she growled. "As you're about to discover. Oh, get up for pity's sake!"

He did so, his hands clutched protectively in front of him, his eyes fixed warily on Dottie. Randolph had been discreetly locating Brenda's robe and helping her put it on. Mike's clothes were scattered about the room, suggesting some urgency in their removal, which did nothing to improve Dottie's temper.

"What are you doing here anyway?" she demanded of Brenda.

"I won a holiday," Brenda said sullenly.

"Oh really!" Dottie turned her fire on Randolph. "Courtesy of the Ellurian Tourist Authority, I suppose? You weren't offered a honeymoon as well, by any chance?"

"None of your business!"

"Oh yes it is," Dottie said wrathfully. "You forget you're talking to the queen."

"Not quite yet—" Randolph murmured.

"You hush!" she told him firmly. "You've told me often enough about my power. Well, how's this for power?" She swung back to the other two. "I could have both of you arrested, locked up and nobody would ever hear of you again."

Brenda gave a little squeak, and Mike edged closer to her. "She can't do it, love," he muttered. "We haven't broken the law."

"Think treason," Dottie suggested dangerously. "Think firing squad."

"Her Royal Highness is naturally disturbed by this breach of protocol," Randolph said smoothly, "and she desires only to find a way out of the unfortunate situation.''

''A firing squad,'' Dottie said stubbornly.

''Aw, c'mon Dot,'' Mike said placatingly. ''You'd finished with me anyhow. You just hadn't gotten around to telling me yet.''

Before she could answer Randolph drew her aside. ''Perhaps you shouldn't blame him too much,'' he murmured. ''After all, you too have permitted yourself—shall we say the odd moment of dalliance?''

She met his eyes and saw in them something that made her gaze fall. He was reminding her of scurrying excitements that he could cause in her, thrills that she'd never known with Mike. They were starting again, reviving the memory of the kiss that had made her feel so guilty. But she'd fled temptation, she remembered. Mike had embraced it full-on.

''That's different,'' she muttered. ''I didn't go in for...what they were doing.''

''Are you sure it might not have happened, if the circumstances had been right?''

''Quite sure.''

His eyes called her a liar. She whirled away from him and confronted Mike, who'd hastily resumed his clothes, and with them, some of his confidence.

''What do you mean by saying I'd finished with you?''

''You've belonged here from the start. And you knew it really. What would you do in Wenford after this? Besides,'' he indicated Randolph who was talking kindly to Brenda, and dropped his voice to say, ''you've gotta marry him.''

''I—he—what are you talking about? I'm marrying

you. At least, I was before you turned out to be a devious, treacherous, unfaithful..."

Mike gave her his sweet smile. "I'm not really, Dot. I'm just an ordinary feller, who wants an ordinary home and an ordinary wife. Thing is, you ain't ordinary."

Randolph returned to them. "The kindest thing you can do for Mike is to let him go back to England, where he can marry Brenda, and settle down with his own garage."

"He hasn't got a garage," Dottie pointed out grumpily.

Randolph held up a set of keys. "These keys unlock the place you had your eye on, Mike. It was purchased last week by the Ellurian embassy, and can be transferred to you whenever you wish, together with a check that I believe will be sufficient for you to make whatever improvements are needed. There is, of course, a condition."

He eyed Mike significantly. Mike eyed Dottie nervously. Reading resignation in her face he changed from nervous to sheepish.

"Sorry, love," he said, accepting the keys. "But it's better this way. You're a smashing lass, but you're like a steamroller." He added confidentially to Randolph, "You'll find that out."

Randolph grinned and nodded.

"I suppose you're going now," Dottie said.

"Well, we're a bit in the way, aren't we?" Mike suggested.

"Yes," Randolph said, "but it has been a pleasure knowing you. A car will take you to the airport. Just pack your immediate necessities. The rest will be sent on."

An historian would have been intrigued by the way Her Royal Highness bid farewell to her victorious rival. But he wouldn't have understood a word.

"You always said you'd have him off me," Dottie said. "I suppose I should have listened. But you be good to him, or you'll have me to deal with."

"Honest Dot, I'll make him happier than you would have."

"Bet you don't!"

"Bet I do!"

"Bet you don't!"

"We'll call our first girl Dottie." Brenda patted her stomach. "She should be settling in nicely by now."

"What?"

"Well, I have been here for two weeks."

"Two—I see." Dottie cast Randolph a look that boded ill for him.

For her final words to Mike she drew him aside, out of earshot of Randolph.

"What were you on about, saying I was marrying Randolph? You're daft, you are."

"No I'm not. Everyone knows he has to marry you so that he can be king, like he was supposed to be. That's what it's all about." He kissed her cheek. "'Bye love. It was great knowing you."

She kissed him back and said goodbye, but by now she was functioning on automatic. Mike's last words were whirling in her head. She'd been brought here to marry Randolph, and everyone knew it, including Randolph.

While Randolph escorted the lovers to the waiting car, Dottie stormed back to her own apartments. None of this was Mike's fault. He'd been *manipulated* into betraying her. Just as she herself had been manipulated.

From her balcony she watched as the car drew away, taking her old life with it. She was here for good now, because she had nothing to go back to. Randolph had seen to that.

As he returned to the building he glanced up at her and she summoned him with a small movement of her head, something that once she would never have done. He arrived a few minutes later, looking like a man bracing himself. "All right. Say it."

"Say it," she seethed. "You mean say it and get it over with, so that you can brush it aside. Because you don't actually mean to take a blind bit of notice."

"I'll do whatever you wish. Shall I fetch Mike back?"

"You know it's too late for that."

"It was always too late," he said flatly.

"Only because you've been pulling strings."

"I didn't force him to make love to Brenda."

"You put her there."

"I put her into his room, not his bed. That was up to him. I suppose he could always have controlled himself."

"She'd been here two weeks," Dottie said, choosing to ignore this. "What a time you must have had keeping us apart, making sure I never suspected anything. Quite a conspiracy. You've been determined to break us up since we arrived."

"Since before that."

She gasped. "You admit it?"

"Why should I deny it? There's no place in your life for Mike. You have to realize that."

"Oh really? Well, maybe being princess has some

hadn't opened my eyes today? What next? Would you have been crass enough to try to make me think you were in love with me? I suppose I should be grateful to have been spared that piece of dishonesty."

He stepped closer to her, his eyes very hard. "Be quiet," he said. "You make your glib judgments and you think you know everything. Try looking at the reality."

"The reality is that you want your throne back and there's only one way of getting it without starting a war," she flashed.

"And you think I'm low enough to cheat and deceive you to get it."

"That's exactly what you did at the start. Mr. Holsson and the tourist authority. You've won a prize to sunny Elluria. I wonder you can look me in the face."

"I did what I had to do," he shouted.

"That's a rotten excuse and you shouldn't hide behind it. You did what suited you and called it duty. That's what being royal means, isn't it?"

"Being royal means doing what you have to, whether it's what you want or not. It means giving up what you love and settling for what you can get."

"So you give up Sophie and settle for me? Do I congratulate you?"

He didn't know how to answer her in this mood. Dottie's eyes warned him to be careful. She was bitterly, wretchedly angry, in a way that was new to him. Where was the chuckling pixie who'd enchanted him? This woman looked as though she'd never laughed in her life.

While he stood there, dumb, she walked away to the window and stood looking out at the avenue of limes. After a moment he went up behind her, and spoke softly.

"Do you remember what you said to me that first evening by the Thames?"

"Don't," she said huskily, putting a hand over her eyes. "Don't ever mention it again."

"I must, because that night you opened your heart and spoke to me out of your true self. You said that you'd dreamed of being a children's nurse. Now I know why. It's in you, that instinct to care for those weaker than yourself. Now you have three million children looking to you. 'A true mother to her people,' they called you. Who will care for your children if you don't?"

"Oh, you know all the right things to say, don't you?" she cried in despair.

"No, it's you that says the right things. I merely remind you of them. That night you spoke of fate and destiny, and how there was a niche waiting for you somewhere in the world, that only you could fill. Those were your very words."

She turned. He met her eyes, hoping to see in them understanding and acceptance, but there was only the dread of a trapped animal.

"Dottie," he said gently, touching her.

But she sprang back at once as though his touch was hateful to her. "Keep away from me," she said hoarsely. "I can't bear to look at you. *Keep away.*"

He put out his hand but he was too late to stop her. She evaded him and darted for the door, then outside, and he heard her footsteps along the corridor. After a moment she appeared on the ground, racing along the long drive where Mike's car had departed, as though she had some wild hope of calling him back. But then she turned aside. Randolph's last view of her was disappearing into the trees.

For an hour Dottie wandered beside the lake, her thoughts too jumbled to make any sense. Sometimes it seemed that she wasn't thinking at all, just feeling. But feeling hurt too much. Randolph was right. It was better to do without it.

She hoped he wouldn't send anyone after her. She needed the solitude of this place, to be away from him. She'd relied on Randolph every moment since she came here, and now she didn't know how she could ever rely on him again.

Looking around, she realized that she was in the place she'd seen from her window the night she came to Elluria. In this spot Randolph had wandered with the woman he loved, his arms around her, thinking himself hidden by the darkness.

It was a long time before she returned to her room. He was no longer there and she sat for a while, not allowing anyone in. Just now she needed solitude. After a while she rang the bell and summoned Aunt Liz.

She had much to keep her occupied for the rest of the day. Her dressmakers brought several half-finished outfits to be fitted and there were decisions to be made. What should she wear for this reception and that? What shoes went with what? She was meeting an ambassador and must wear the jewels that had been a gift from his country.

It was strange how rivetingly interesting new clothes could be one day, and how depressing another.

It was silly to quarrel, she thought, as her anger

evaporated. This was what he'd meant when he'd talked about realpolitik. It was the real world of royalty.

She didn't like this world. It was a place where she was expected to marry Randolph and be satisfied with the outward show; a world where her heart and feelings had no place.

But she couldn't afford to be at odds with her chief advisor. She would smooth it over somehow. She called his room on the internal phone, and his valet answered.

"Prince Randolph isn't here," he said. "He left the palace some hours ago to visit his estate. Do I understand that he left without informing Your Royal Highness? Oh dear."

"No," she said quickly. "He did mention it of course. I forgot."

"Do you wish him to be notified that his presence is required?"

"No, that won't be necessary."

As she went to bed that night Aunt Liz mentioned that she'd left her "a little light reading," on her table. This proved to be a scholarly history of Elluria, and a reference book on the country's constitution.

She discovered that the sovereign's power was considerable. Elluria had an elected parliament from which most of the cabinet were drawn. But she could appoint anyone as a minister, elected or not. Also she could, at any time, declare a state of emergency and rule by decree. No wonder she scared them. She scared herself.

Now more than ever she needed Randolph here to explain everything and reassure her. But he was also the last person she would trust, because it all added up to a reason why she should marry him.

And pigs would fly first.

Next day Aunt Liz was bubbling over with excitement.

"Are the rumors really true? You're going to stay? Oh, that's wonderful!"

Dottie was touched by the older woman's obvious delight. But perhaps Liz was only pleased because she foresaw a marriage. A different candidate might have been a man, or already married, leaving Randolph out in the cold.

Was this what it meant to be a queen? To be suspicious of everyone who was nice to you? If so, it was a bleak prospect. And now there was nobody to help her. She was truly alone. The aloneness of royalty.

She soon realized that the news that she was staying had changed everything. Now she must appoint ladies in waiting, meet her cabinet and have in-depth discussions with her prime minister.

About what for heavens sake? Somebody tell me what I'm supposed to be doing.

"Of course you met your chief ministers when you arrived," Aunt Liz reminded her. "But today it will be the full cabinet. I think your clothes should be slightly severe, your hair up, just one piece of jewelry, this brooch that bears the coat of arms of Elluria."

As she dressed for her first cabinet meeting Dottie's thoughts swung about like a pendulum.

He's left me like this to show me that I can't manage without him. I didn't think he'd descend to that.

It seems I got him wrong. Well, he got me wrong too. Do I need him?

The meeting was in the parliament building, in the city. At noon Dottie was ready, pale but determined. She heard the faint knock at the outer door, but barely registered it until Bertha hurried in to say, "Prince Randolph asks leave to attend you, ma'am."

She discovered that she could assume the royal mask, so that nobody could suspect the way her heart leapt. Nor did her voice quaver as she said, "Please ask him to enter," although she was trembling inside.

Randolph looked like a man who'd spent a desperate, sleepless night. Dottie had meant to stay angry with him but she couldn't. In another moment she would have opened her arms, apologized for her angry words and asked him to be friends again. But before she could do so he bowed and said, "I am at Your Royal Highness's service."

His cool politeness was more hurtful than a slap in the face. He was doing his duty. No more.

"I thought you would be away for several days," she said quietly.

"Forgive me for leaving without first informing you," he responded. "That was improper of me."

She wanted to cry out, *Don't talk to me like that. This is me, Dottie.*

But it was too late. There was no going back to the old days: happy days, she understood, now that they were gone.

"Are you coming with me to the cabinet meeting?" she asked.

"If that is what you wish."

"I can't manage it without you."

"Then I shall certainly be there. It won't be very

terrible. Remember they're more nervous of you than you of them."

"Impossible."

"You can dismiss them at will and appoint your own nominee."

"Yes, that's what the book said. It doesn't sound very democratic."

"It isn't, but it can be very effective."

"Then why don't I just appoint you prime minister? That would be fair, wouldn't it?"

It was a mistake. If possible his face closed against her even more firmly, and his voice seemed to come from an arctic cave.

"It would be far from fair to dismiss Jacob Durmand, one of the best prime ministers this country has ever had. Nor do I wish to be the subject of your charity. I trust I make myself clear."

"Perfectly. Shall we go?"

"Wait one moment," he said imperiously. "There are things to be said between us first."

"You're angry about what I said yesterday, but—"

She stopped, for Randolph had held up his hand as if warding her off. He didn't deny that he was angry, she noticed. He merely consigned the subject to the realms of the unimportant—as feelings were, to him, she reminded herself.

"Listen to me," he said quietly. "And heed what I say, for I have never been more serious in my life. Once you've attended that meeting, you're committed, finally and irrevocably to the people—*your* people. After today a door will slam shut behind you."

"Oh no. The door slammed shut yesterday. You must have noticed. You did it."

"I think it could be opened again. You could return to England, reclaim Mike."

"How could I ever do that?"

Randolph put his fingers beneath her chin and lifted it. "Remember what you told me once? 'A smile usually does it.' In London I watched you turn the chef into your slave. And Fritz in the kitchens here—he'd lay down and die for you. You have the gift of winning hearts, Dottie. You could win Mike's back. You could win...any man's." The last words seemed to come from him reluctantly.

She scanned his face in wonder at this strange talk. His expression was gentle, but beyond that she couldn't read.

For a moment the temptation dazzled her. To regain all she'd lost and return to her contented life.

Then reality kicked in and she gave a little sigh. "It's no use. Mike never really loved me. He just thought he did because—" she gave a jerky little laugh, "because I kept telling him. Like he said, I'm a steamroller."

"A sovereign needs to be a bit of a steamroller. But she also needs the gift of winning hearts, which you have. I'll help you all I can, but you must give me your word that you're totally committed. We can accept nothing less."

"We?"

"Your subjects," he said quietly.

"But—"

"That's what we are," he interrupted her. "Every one of us. We've given you our hearts, and all we ask in return is—everything. Your life, your freedom, your independence, your time. We ask you to think of us day and night, to put us first no matter what your own feelings dictate. In other words, we ask your love.''

''Everything,'' she whispered.

''Yes, it's a lot to ask. This is your last chance to escape. After today there's no going back.''

Dottie gave a wry smile. ''There never really was, was there?''

''No. There never really was.''

She put her hand in his.

''I think we should go now,'' she said. ''They're waiting for us.''

Chapter Eight

Two cars left the palace for the parliament building. In the second was Aunt Liz and another lady-in-waiting. The leading vehicle was a black limousine that had been specially constructed for the purpose of transporting a monarch. The entire rear was one huge window made of bulletproof glass, so that the sovereign should be easily visible.

Dottie sat there by herself. Randolph had chosen to sit in the front, beside the chauffeur, and by now she was sufficiently attuned to protocol to understand that this detail was significant. On this important day her people would see her alone.

She couldn't know that Randolph had another reason. He sat apart from her because he needed time to sort out the turmoil of his feelings.

Dottie's harsh judgment of him had briefly been right. He'd left the palace in a mood of bitterness, and headed for his estate, meaning to stay there. Dottie's mistrust, her accusations that he'd acted from base motives, infuriated him, and the look on her face when she'd said "I can't bear to look at you," had struck him like a blow. He'd put as much distance between them as he could.

But he'd barely arrived at his country house when his more generous self reclaimed him. He'd brought her here, dumped her in the middle of a crisis and then abandoned her. And why? Because his pride was hurt. He, who'd always said that feelings didn't count beside his duty to his country, had done something so cruel.

He'd spent the night pacing the floor, and next day he'd returned to the palace, arriving just in time. He'd searched her face as he entered, for any sign that she was pleased to see him, but her manner had all the regal austerity that he'd tried to teach her. It should have been a triumphant moment.

Now they were entering Wolfenberg, drawing up before the parliament building, an elaborate edifice that looked incongruously like a wedding cake on the outside. But inside it was redolent of history. Tapestries, depicting battles, hung on the walls. Statues of monarchs stood gloomily in niches. Red tiles streamed across the floors.

In a small chamber that led directly to the cabinet room Randolph said to Dottie, "Would you oblige me by waiting here a moment, while I go in first, to make sure everything is in order for you?"

She nodded and he strode into the next room. The ministers were already in place, and they greeted him with relief.

"If you're going to direct proceedings, sir, we'll

all be very relieved,'' Sternheim announced. He was one of the few who hadn't warmed to Dottie.

''I'm not,'' Randolph announced flatly. ''And you must put any such thought out of your head.''

There was a universal groan.

''A woman,'' Sternheim said. ''And a stupid, ignorant foreigner at that.''

''Keep your voice down,'' Randolph snapped. ''That is exactly the kind of attitude I came to warn you about.''

''Be assured we shall observe all proper respect,'' Durmand said soothingly.

''I meant more than that,'' Randolph told him. ''Let me tell you something about your crown princess. She might be naive but she isn't stupid, especially about people. Don't ever make the mistake of underestimating her, because she'll pounce on any slip you make like a ferret up a drainpipe.''

Sternheim was aghast. ''Like a what?''

''Never mind,'' Randolph said hastily. He didn't know what had made him say that, except that Dottie's rich language had come back to him suddenly, and it was catching.

Next door Dottie walked up and down, increasingly nervous at the delay. Aunt Liz had opened the door a crack and was shamelessly eavesdropping.

Dottie couldn't bring herself to do the same but ''stupid, ignorant foreigner'' reached her clearly.

''If he just went in there to stir them up he needn't have bothered,'' she muttered.

''Of course not,'' Aunt Liz said. ''He's trying to ensure that they show you respect.''

''Then he's doing a lousy job. And I'll fight my own battles,'' she added illogically.

At last Randolph returned, to lead her into the cabinet room. It was lined with bookshelves weighed down by learned-looking tomes. In the center was a heavy table, large enough to seat fourteen people. Randolph led her to her seat, and when he had solemnly presented her he stepped back and to the side, moving his chair to where she could just see him out of the corner of her eye.

Durmand gave a speech of welcome, then he courteously asked if she had anything to say to her ministers.

"Yes," she said. "I have. Please sit."

When they were all seated she felt horribly exposed, the only one on her feet. Until today it had been a kind of game. Suddenly it was for real.

"I think none of us really expected this moment to come," she said in a voice that surprised her by being steady. "I thought you would find somebody more suitable, and you must certainly have hoped for it."

Perceiving that their sovereign had made a witticism the ministers permitted themselves a few smiles.

"But here we are, and must make the best of each other," she continued. "I know I can rely on your loyalty both to me, and to Elluria. And you can rely on my loyalty to my new country."

That pleased them and she was able to smile as she seated herself, asking, "What do we do now?"

It seemed there were many matters requiring her attention. Since it was her prerogative to appoint the cabinet every minister resigned and was immediately reappointed.

"But I may wish to make a few changes later," Dottie observed. "I notice that there are no women here."

''There are only six women in parliament,'' Sternheim noted caustically.

''And how many men?'' Dottie wanted to know.

Sternheim gave a snort of impatience. ''I don't recall the precise figure.''

''But you're my chancellor. If such a simple sum is beyond you, perhaps I should think again.''

There were smothered smiles. Sternheim snapped. ''Eighty-two.''

''And only six women? Well, there'll be time for me to put that right.''

Bernhard Enderlin, minister of the Interior, coughed gently. ''Strictly speaking, ma'am, that's my province.''

''Certainly it is,'' Dottie agreed warmly. ''I look forward to discussing it with you. Shall we say sometime next week? That will give you time to work out your plan. How lucky that I'm here.''

''I see that you believe in taking the bull by the horns, ma'am,'' Enderlin said, accepting defeat with grace.

''Otherwise known as being a steamroller,'' Dottie murmured. ''Is there any other business?''

''The Korburg ambassador is agitating for his master to be invited for a private visit,'' Enderlin said. ''It hardly seems advisable in the circumstances.''

''I disagree,'' Dottie said at once. ''Do you want him to think you're so unsure of me that you're hiding me from him? Nothing could be more dangerous. Never mind a private visit. Let's invite him for a *state* visit.''

There was consternation around the table.

''The more fuss the better,'' Dottie rattled on before anyone could speak. "Let him *see* that the throne of Elluria is occupied. That'll teach him."

Consternation changed to smiles as her meaning got through, and there were murmurs of approval.

"Bull by the horns, gentlemen," Dottie said. "Boldness is best. Harold and I can get a good look at each other. He'll spit feathers, I'll say 'Get knotted!' and that will be that. All right, don't faint any of you. I'll just smile sweetly and do my stuff."

Everyone sighed with relief. Durmand, seeming to feel that the sooner the meeting ended the better for everyone's nerves, murmured, "In that case..."

"One moment," Dottie stopped him. "I have another appointment to make. You all know how unprepared I am for all this. Some people think I'm no more than a 'stupid, ignorant foreigner.'" She waited for the nervous frisson to die down. Out of the corner of her eye she saw Randolph give a faint smile. "Maybe I am, but it's not all I am, and to prove that I need help. Nobody can help me better than Prince Randolph, which is why," she took a deep breath, "I'm asking him to be my confidential, private secretary."

There were smiles of pleasure and relief. Dottie turned to Randolph, expecting to see approval, perhaps even a smile, but at once she knew she'd misread him. Of everyone in the room, he alone was not pleased, although good manners prevented him from saying so. He inclined his head and murmured something about wishing only to serve her, but his heart wasn't in it.

On the journey home he joined her in the back, shutting the partition so that they could speak privately.

"You had no right to do that without consulting me first," he growled.

"I only thought of it at the last minute. Besides, it's perfect. You can keep me from making mistakes."

"Like the one you just made?"

"I'm sorry for the way I did it, but that's all."

"Then let me give you my first piece of advice as your confidential, private secretary. Don't ever, *ever* take me by surprise again."

His reaction gave her a sense of disappointment that cut sharply and made her snap back, "I'm the crown princess. I can do anything I like."

"Not anything."

"Yes, anything. If you don't believe me, read the constitution. And if you say another word I'll declare a state of emergency."

That silenced him. They spoke little on the way back to the palace, and Dottie had supper alone, feeling let down. She confided in Aunt Liz, and was surprised when the older woman seemed troubled.

"You don't think I did the right thing?"

"It depends what you were trying to tell people," Aunt Liz said cautiously. "Naturally you need Randolph at your side, but people were thinking… That is they hoped—"

"That I would marry him? Suppose I don't want to?"

"Then the sensible option is to keep him by you as a servant. Which is what you've done."

Dottie's hand flew to her mouth in horror. "A servant? Oh no! That's not what I meant at all. I meant to honor him."

"You think he's honored to be a secretary? A royal

prince? Not that he's a royal prince now. Or any kind of prince.''

''What is he then?'' Dottie asked curiously. ''Surely he has some other titles?''

''He lost all his titles since he was illegitimate.''

''What, everything? And what about his estate? I know he still has that.''

''That was a personal gift from his father years ago, so it's safe. But it's all he has now, and it's a very small place. Just a retreat, really.'' She considered Dottie before saying casually, ''Of course, you could always make him a prince again. Not a royal prince, and it wouldn't make him legitimate, but you could give him a courtesy title that would make his life a lot easier.''

''Did he ask you to suggest that?''

''Oh my dear, if you haven't understood that he'd go to the stake rather than ask, even indirectly, then you haven't begun to understand him.''

''No, I suppose I don't understand him. But he doesn't want me to, I understand that much. He'd see it as a sort of invasion. Oh heavens! I've done it all wrong. I'm always going to do everything wrong. Why didn't I think? Because I never think. I'm an idiot, a clown. I have no right to be here. Oh *damn!*''

Of the twelve candidates to be her ladies-in-waiting, the only one Dottie knew was Jeanie, Countess Batz, whom she'd met when they'd all gone to the nightclub. The others had briefly passed before her and been lost in a blur. Dottie immediately picked her.

''A good choice as a lady-in-waiting,'' Aunt Liz

enthused, "although perhaps a little young to be your *chief* lady."

"I suppose I'll see more of the chief lady than the others?"

"Certainly."

"Then I'll have Jeanie. I like her. Besides, her English is perfect."

"They all speak perfect English," Randolph remarked from a nearby table, where he was making notes. He didn't raise his head or look at her.

"I want Jeanie," Dottie said stubbornly.

"As Your Royal Highness commands," Aunt Liz agreed.

"Oh, don't give me that," Dottie said crisply. "I did exactly what the two of you meant me to do. I'll bet you put your heads together and said, 'How can we make her choose Jeanie for chief lady? Oh yes, tell her Jeanie's unsuitable and watch her take the bait.' You were like a pair of sheepdogs corralling me into the pen."

They were both looking at her now. She looked back, not defiantly but evenly, like a businesswoman setting out her terms. "Okay, it worked. Just don't kid yourself that I didn't see it happening. I may be ditzy but I'm not daft."

"Of course you're not," Liz enthused. "That's just what Randolph told your ministers. 'Like a ferret up a drainpipe,' he said."

"Did he indeed?" Dottie murmured. "How interesting. It seems I'm not the only one learning things."

Randolph gathered his papers and prepared to depart, but paused beside her first to murmur, "Well done, ma'am. You're getting good at the game."

"You mean the game of never trusting anyone?"

she murmured back. "Yes, I was sorry to learn that one, but I manage better now that I have."

She met Randolph's eyes. His fell first. These days it seemed that every conversation between them ended in some awkwardness. The gap between them yawned, unbridgeable, heartbreaking.

But Dottie was getting good at the nuances of court life. When she made her next move it was carefully planned.

She had just taken part in her first investiture. In front of a small audience twenty people came before her, bent one leg onto a small stool so that they were half-kneeling, and just the right height for her to pin on a medal, or bestow a title.

Randolph stood beside her, telling her who each one was, and how they had deserved honor, and when it was over and they were walking back to her apartments, she said casually, "Harold will be here soon. I'm working hard to learn everything I need to know, but I'm still floundering. Never mind. You'll be there to look after me all the time, won't you?"

"I'm afraid not," he said.

"But why?" she asked in apparent surprise, although she already knew the answer.

"Because I'm only your secretary, and you can't keep me by you on state occasions. Naturally I'll help you behind the scenes—"

"No good. I want you 'on stage' with me."

"That honor belongs to someone from a titled family. This is a very old-fashioned court, still. Tradition prevails. Only those of the highest rank may attend the monarch in public."

"Then the solution's easy. I just restore your titles. Plus all," she began to quote frantically before she could forget, "appurtenances and privileges thereto-fore, not withstanding, herinafter, thingywhatsit and howsyourfather."

His lips twitched. "You've been doing your home-work very well."

"And landed estates," she finished triumphantly.

"No, that you can't do. They are crown heritage and must belong to you. But the rest—" he broke off, sorely tempted.

Then he remembered the ceremony he'd just wit-nessed. He thought of kneeling before her; he who'd kneeled to nobody in his life, and his pride revolted. He was about to tell her stiffly that he would prefer not to receive her charity, but he saw her watching him anxiously, and realized how hard she'd worked to make this easy for him. His heart softened.

"Thank you, ma'am," he said gravely. "It's a kind offer, and I accept."

Her smile of relief told him how nervous she'd been of his reaction, and he was shocked at himself. He couldn't match her generosity. He could only pre-tend to and hope she didn't suspect.

She arranged the ceremony so quickly that he guessed she'd had everything planned. There was a small crowd, a few of the highest ranking families, the women in evening gowns and jewels, the men ablaze with decorations. Dottie was glittering with di-amonds from the crown jewels, retrieved from the bank that morning under armed guard.

Randolph himself was in full dress uniform and Dottie, watching him walk toward her, thought he'd never looked so splendid. She knew this must be pain-ful for him, but if only he would smile at her they could share the moment and turn the pain aside.

But he gave her no smile. His face remained stern and set as he neared the steps that led up to the throne, beside which she was standing. He climbed the steps, his eyes searching for the stool on which he must bend the knee.

It wasn't there.

His eyes met hers, registering his surprise that this detail had been forgotten. Then he saw her smile, saw her shake her head slightly and understood that this was no accident. The next moment she confirmed it, reaching out her hand to draw him to stand at her side.

She began to read from the letters patent that returned his status. Inwardly Randolph flinched, waiting for the words, "our loyal and most devoted servant." It was foolish to be so troubled by a few words, after what he'd already endured, but every pinprick seemed to pierce him twice now.

She was nearly there. As if from a distance he heard Dottie say, "our loyal and most devoted cousin and friend..."

A frisson went around the crowd. She'd departed from the traditional words of the letters patent, words that had been carved in stone for centuries. She'd simply dumped them to spare the feelings of the man beside her. Randolph stared at Dottie, shock warring with gratitude.

Next moment she had another shock for him. Refusing to let him kiss her hand she reached up and kissed his cheek. Then she took his hand and gestured to the applauding crowd, presenting him to them, inviting them to share her pleasure.

Randolph was aware of a dangerous ache in his throat. It mustn't happen. He had to speak. Somehow he managed it. The discipline held, the words came out, meaningless because all he was aware of was Dottie's hand still holding his.

It was over. He turned, went down the steps and walked away. But before he did so he tightened his hand on hers and felt the answering grasp of her fingers. They felt so small against his big hand, but their grip was surprisingly strong.

That was how they communicated these days; through public gestures filled with unspoken emotion, while their private conversations were awkward and uneasy.

Everyone agreed that inviting Harold for a state visit had been a brilliant idea, but it resulted in Dottie needing a crash course in "royal" behavior.

She, who'd never been to a formal dinner in her life, must become familiar with a whole array of cutlery, wineglasses, finger bowls. That was the easy part. It was the conversation that drove her distracted.

"Can't I just smile and say, 'My, how interesting'?" she begged.

"Certainly," Jeanie agreed. She'd entered into her new duties, and her youth and fun-loving nature were just what Dottie needed.

"You can say, 'My how interesting' when you're visiting a hospital or meeting a line of actors after the theater," she explained now. "But in a longer conversation it's not enough. You have to introduce a new topic now and then."

"But why can't other people do that?" Dottie demanded distractedly. "Then I could just float with the tide, and say 'My, how interesting!' at short intervals."

"Because only you can change the subject."

"*What?*"

"Nobody but you can introduce a new topic. If the sovereign wants to discuss one-legged spiders all night then that's what everyone has to do."

"I'm outta here."

"Now don't panic."

"Panic? I'm in a state of stark terror. You're all crazy."

The other thing she had trouble with was the royal "we."

"You're not just one person," Randolph explained. "You represent the state. In fact, you *are* the state. So you're speaking for both of you."

"Both of who?"

"You and the state."

"But you just said I *was* the state. So that's just one of us, isn't it?"

"In a sense. But you are you and the state is the state."

"Except that I'm the state, and the state is me."

To her surprise he beamed. "Excellent Dottie. Louis XIV expressed it in those very words. *L'etat c'est moi!*"

"Why didn't he speak English?"

"Because he was French."

She tore her hair. "How did he get into this conversation?"

"Because you used the very same words, thus proving that you really do belong in the great line-up of rulers. Just remember, you use the royal 'we' to indicate that you speak for your country as well."

"But I'll sound daft saying, 'We would like another slice of toast.' I'll probably end up with two."

Randolph closed his eyes. "It's only for use in public," he said with difficulty. "'We are delighted to declare that…' or 'It is our wish that…' And so on."

"Okay, I'll try to get the hang of it. Now, would you mind going because it's late and *we* would like to do our toenails before *we* go to bed?"

In between learning the proprieties, she interested herself in politics in a way that set her ministers' nerves jangling. At the earliest possible date she carried out her threat to summon Enderlin to discuss the low number of women in parliament.

"There really is nothing to be done about it," he protested. "Women aren't applying to stand for seats."

"But they might if the hours weren't so long," said Dottie, who'd been studying hard. "If you reorganized the debates so that the votes were at a reasonable hour I think the women would come forward." After a moment's thought she mused, "With a little encouragement."

Enderlin turned a hunted look on Randolph who was sitting to one side, but he seemed preoccupied with his notes.

"Do I understand that you intend to provide the encouragement, ma'am?" Enderlin asked faintly.

"Could be."

"Might I suggest that these interventions would be more appropriate when you've been here a little longer?"

"You mean when the election's over?" Dottie asked mischievously. "I did know that there was one due in a year. I want things done before that."

He made one last effort. "Such matters take time—"

"Not if you have the power of decree," Dottie reminded him mischievously. "We'll have to move fast if we're to get things changed before then, but I know I can leave that to you. Randolph is always telling me how efficient you are."

When Enderlin had bowed himself out Randolph said grimly, "Do you mind leaving me out of your assaults on the executive? I value my skin."

"Coward."

"Yes, I am a coward," he said after a moment. "More than you know, ma'am."

"Don't call me that."

"It is appropriate."

"I mean when we're alone. I'm still Dottie." There was almost a plea in her words.

"No," he said at last. "Dottie has gone a long way away, and how can I complain? It was I who sent her away."

He walked out without the usual punctilious request for permission, leaving her wanting to burst into tears. Or throw something. Either one would have been better than the ache she felt all the time nowadays, and which she'd soon realized had nothing to do with the loss of Mike. It was the loss of Randolph that hurt.

It had been building up since that night in London when he'd whisked her away from her ordinary life, thrown magic into the air so that it dazzled her as it fell, and then…

"And then he made me fall in love with him," she mused. "Dirty, rotten swine!"

Her feelings for him had always been there, from the first evening. No, from the first moment when she'd seen him in the café and known that he was unlike all other men. He was thrilling and dangerous, and he'd aroused her senses as Mike never had. She'd called him a magician, too ignorant and unsuspecting to know that the spell he cast was the oldest one in the world.

She would have seen the truth earlier if there hadn't been so many things in the way. But she saw it now, and it made her so angry with him that sometimes she could hardly bear to be with him. But when she wasn't with him it was worse.

Most painful of all was the knowledge that she could marry him tomorrow. A man as shrewd and subtle as Randolph would know the right words to convince her, because she longed to be convinced. Just let him once guess her feelings for him, and she would be lost. They would embark on a marriage of love on her side and duty on his. And in no time at all she would hate him.

Sophie had left the palace now and was living at the Bekendorf family mansion in Wolfenberg, at which, it was rumored, a stream of gifts arrived each day from Korburg. But she still had the freedom of the palace park, and arrived there most mornings for a ride.

Sometimes Randolph joined her, for it suited his pride to have the world see that they were still on good terms. And Sophie, still doing a hopeful juggling act, always welcomed him warmly.

One morning when he didn't appear she went to seek him out in his office. Strictly speaking she should have been properly announced before walking in on the crown princess's private secretary while he was reading the royal correspondence. But while Sophie stuck rigidly to protocol for others, she blithely ignored it to suit herself.

"My dear," Randolph said, rising to kiss her cheek. "It's good to see you looking so well."

She was at her best, blazing with life and health, and elegant in her riding habit. She kissed him back, cheekily, on the mouth, lingering just a moment too long, so that he gently disengaged himself.

"Prince Harold would not approve," he said lightly.

She shrugged. "Oh, nothing's settled. But he'll be here soon."

"Sophie be careful," he said, meaning only to be kind. "Harold is a cold, unscrupulous man. He won't treat you well if it suits him not to."

"Whatever do you mean?"

"I mean he may be after bigger fish. He still wants the throne of Elluria."

"As do you," she said with a brittle laugh. "You'd better marry the silly creature quickly before she realizes what you're really after."

"Don't talk like that," he said in a voice he'd never used to her before. "I forbid you ever to mention the subject again. It's an insult to her and an insult to me."

Sophie shrugged, not disconcerted, as Dottie would have been, by the bleak winter that had come over Randolph. She'd miscalculated, but she would recover. She perched on a corner of his desk and glanced over the letters there. Randolph didn't notice, being occupied in arranging coffee for her, to atone for his ill temper. By the time he dismissed the servant and looked back into the room Sophie was tearing open a small packet.

"What are you doing?" he demanded. "You can't open her letters."

"Why not? It's from England. You couldn't have given it to her anyway. It's probably from her lover. Read it and throw it away."

Examining the wrapping Randolph saw, with a sinking heart, that it was postmarked Wenford.

Sophie gave a shriek of laughter. "Listen to this...'Dottie, love—'"

"Give me that," Randolph snapped, tearing it from her hands. "How the devil am I going to explain to her that it's been opened?"

"I thought it was your job."

"Not her private letters."

"She shouldn't be getting private letters from her lover. Just don't give it to her."

"I shall give it to her, because I won't betray her trust."

"She wouldn't know."

"She would if you grew careless and—shall we say?—let it slip."

"*Me?* Do such a thing?"

"I'm not sure, but I'm beginning to realize that I never really knew you Sophie." He gave her a level gaze that would have alarmed a more perceptive woman. "Perhaps you and Harold will go well together after all."

She smiled. "Don't you think I'll make a splendid Princess Consort?"

"Only for him. Not for me. I don't think you should come here again."

There was no mistaking his meaning. Sophie scowled, understanding that this game, at least, was lost.

"I'll leave you then," she snapped, snatching up her riding hat and marching out so forcefully that the servant, bringing coffee, was forced to flatten himself against the doorjamb.

Chapter Nine

Left alone with the letter in his hands Randolph clenched his fingers slowly so that the paper was scrunched and only *Dottie, love* was showing.

It wasn't too bad, he told himself. Mike might have written "My darling," or something intense. On second thoughts, no. Intensity wasn't his style. For him, "Dottie, love" was the height of passionate abandon. And she would understand it that way.

If he gave it to her.

He shut off the thought at once. She'd already made it insultingly clear that she didn't trust him. This would simply prove her right, and if she didn't know it, he would.

Without further delay he went to her apartments, marching in without waiting to be announced. Dottie had been contentedly munching breakfast, wrapped in a large pink toweling robe. She choked over her coffee and drew the robe more firmly around her. Her movement was just fast enough to leave him in doubt whether she was wearing anything underneath.

Inwardly he cursed the bitter fate that had made her a sexy imp who could get under his skin without trying to. What was a man to do who'd had one glimpse of the loveliest body on earth, and then been haunted by it, day and night, ever since. The sight was there in his dreams, and with it a rich chuckle at some absurdity of life that he'd never noticed before, but would never forget now, because it reminded him of her. He would awaken to find himself trembling, aching in his loins with a deprivation that only one thing could ease. And that was something he couldn't have.

By day it was even worse, for he would be with her, always at a disadvantage, struggling not to let her suspect feelings that shocked him because he couldn't master them. A lifetime of discipline and control, all set at nothing because this exasperating creature had a smile of wine and honey and a wicked gleam in her eyes. But she hadn't overcome him yet, and he would make sure she didn't.

He coped by keeping their meetings brief, businesslike and sometimes harsh on his side. It frustrated him, but it was his only protection.

"Do you mind?" Dottie asked belligerently.

"I shan't disturb you for long. I merely wished to give you this," he held out the letter, "and to apologize for the error which led to it being opened. It fell in with all the other official correspondence."

"Oh yeah?" she said, looking at the postmark. "You saw Wenford and assumed it was 'official correspondence'?"

"It was an accident, ma'am, but one for which I wish to apologize."

Dottie was examining the rest of the packet, which turned out to contain a piece of wedding cake, and some wedding photos.

"He didn't waste much time," she murmured. "Nice of him to send me some cake."

"May I suggest that letters from your ex-fiancé are inappropriate?" he said, putting as much frozen propriety into the words as he could manage.

She didn't answer at first. She was studying a picture of the bride and groom, happily lost in each other. Looking over her shoulder Randolph felt nauseated by Mike's gaze of foolish fondness for the commonplace creature he'd preferred to the magical Dottie. It made no difference that he himself had pushed them together. Mike should have treasured his enchanting fiancée, and never looked at another woman, no matter what the provocation.

Dottie's face bore a look of sadness. "They look very happy together," she said wistfully.

"Would it have been that way with you and him?" Randolph couldn't stop himself asking.

"Oh no, you were right about that. And he was right, too. She suits him better. It's just, they're daft about each other, like people should be on their wedding day," she added wistfully.

"You speak like someone who's given up on happiness."

"On that kind, yes. You shouldn't be surprised. You brought me to a place where it doesn't happen anymore."

He knew his next words were unwise but all the wisdom in the world couldn't have stopped him saying them. "That's not true Dottie. This can be a happy place."

"It'll never be happy for me," she said quietly.

There was an ache in her voice that he couldn't bear. He would have given anything, if only she could smile again. But she was looking into the distance, murmuring, "A cozy little home and a cozy little husband. This place isn't cozy."

"No, it's not. But as I told you before, you're meant for something bigger."

"It's all right, I'm not fighting anymore. At least, I'm not fighting my destiny, or whatever you want to call it."

"Then what?"

"You. I'll always fight you."

"Because you don't trust me?"

"Because I thought I *could* trust you, before I discovered that I couldn't. That's worse than knowing from the start. But it doesn't matter, does it? Because feelings don't matter and people don't matter."

"I never thought I'd hear you talking like this. I don't like it."

"Well you did it," she said with a little sigh. "I learned my lesson well, didn't I? But this—" she held up the letter and an edge returned to her voice, "this is out of order. Don't you ever dare read my private letters again."

Her swift change from wistful to autocratic caused a revulsion of feeling in him. "I did not read your letter," he said, tight-lipped.

"Oh yeah? You opened it and you didn't read it?"

"I didn't—" He stopped, realizing that the truth would lead to more trouble.

''Didn't what?'' Light dawned. ''You didn't open it? Then who did.''

''It was an accident.''

''Who opened it?''

''Sophie,'' he said unwillingly. ''She was trying to help. She didn't know—''

''You let Sophie read my correspondence?''

''I didn't mean it to happen.''

''Oh please!'' she said bitterly. ''Did I give the pair of you a good laugh?''

''Don't call me a liar,'' he said in a dangerously quiet voice. ''Don't ever do that.''

''You're saying that you haven't read one word of this letter?''

''Only the first two, which strike me as highly unsuitable for you to receive from your ex-lover and a married man. If that had fallen into the wrong hands—''

''As far as I'm concerned it already has.''

''She only saw the start, I'm sure of it.''

''Yes,'' Dottie said in a strange voice, ''Now I'm sure of it, too.'' She was reading the letter. ''I think you should hear this.''

''There's no need,'' he said tensely. ''I don't want to know what passes between you.'' If only this were true!

''Oh, but I think you should hear every word,'' Dottie said, with a light in her eye that troubled him. ''Then you can tell me how 'unsuitable' it is for me to receive it.'' She began to read. ''Dottie love, thought you'd like to know the end of the story. Wedding went off great. Hope you like the cake. Garage is smashing. Am definitely pregnant. Love from 'all three' of us. Best, Brenda.''

When she'd finished there was silence. Randolph looked at her while his reactions warred in him. He felt foolish for having been so completely caught out, but greater still was the feeling of joy. She wasn't exchanging love letters with Mike.

But he couldn't read her. He knew Dottie's gift for "seeing the funny side," but would it rise to this?

"I think perhaps I'll publish this in the court circular," she said with grim hilarity, "so that everyone can see what an efficient secretary I have."

He gave a small, formal bow. "That, of course, is Your Royal Highness's privilege."

"Don't you dare talk to me like that!"

"Well, anything I say or do now is going to be wrong, isn't it?"

"And stop trying to cut the ground out from under my feet."

"I had it cut out pretty comprehensively under mine. Let's face it, Dottie, the joke's on me. Why not just enjoy it?"

As the import of these words dawned on her she felt her anger drain away out of the soles of her feet. It was unbelievable, impossible. "Randolph, are you actually going to stand there and tell me that you've seen a joke against yourself? *You?*"

"I suppose I am. It must be your influence." His lips twitched. "I'm sorry, Dottie. I really am."

"So you should be. Oh heavens!" She finally yielded to her laughter, and he joined in. Laughing at himself was a new experience, but he found he got the hang of it fairly easily.

"That's better," she said. "You see, you can do it." She put her hands on his shoulders and gave him a little shake, and the next moment he'd enfolded her in a bear hug.

"Dottie, Dottie..." He scarcely knew what he was saying, only that it was wonderful to hold her close in a moment of affectionate companionship.

If he tried hard he could believe that was all it was, but in no time he knew it had been a mistake to hold her against his body. The toweling robe was thick, but not thick enough to make him unaware of her nakedness beneath, or to stop him responding to it. He began the movement that would push her away, but it turned to a caress so light that he hoped she wouldn't feel it.

Dottie was so happy to have gotten rid of the hostility between them that she tightened her arms, hugging him with all her might. In return she thought she felt the lightest touch on the top of her head, as though a kiss had been dropped there. She looked up quickly, finding his face just above hers, and it seemed to her fancy that he looked like a man who'd just kissed someone and wanted to do so again. He was trembling, but not as hard as she was.

But then his hands were firm on her shoulders, pushing her away. "I'm sure you have a busy day ahead, ma'am."

"No I haven't. I've got a free morning. Let's go riding."

Her eyes were wide and hopeful, full of an offer to forget their quarrel, and return to the time when they had been at ease. Wouldn't a good secretary accept that offer and be on friendly terms with his future sovereign? For the sake of the country?

The temptation hung before him, dazzling him with offers of beauty and excitement: to ride with her under the trees, to walk beside the water where she'd once kissed him, in the days when he'd still been blind to what was so clear now, to laugh and be happy and forget duty.

With a sigh he came down to earth. She was dangerous. She threatened his control.

"It sounds lovely, but your secretary must spend the day serving your interests."

"Oh, all right. Spoilsport. Now push off while I get dressed."

"Of course." He extended his hand. "Friends?"

She took it. "Friends."

It came nowhere near the truth, but it would have to do for now.

The state visit was arranged for six weeks ahead. While preparations went on behind the scenes Dottie's ministers decided to capitalize on her growing popularity by introducing her to the country. She found her schedule full of visits to hospitals, factories, schools.

Often she had to stay overnight. These were fun occasions that she used to get to know her ladies, who were mostly young and lively. The exception was Duchess Alicia Gellin, an elderly widow with a reputation as a battle-ax. Dottie's sharp eyes saw the loneliness beneath the crusty surface, and insisted on appointing her.

It turned out to be an inspired choice. Alicia knew more gossip than the rest of the court put together, and she kept Dottie in the know better than any security service.

On one hospital visit she outlined the timetable, ten minutes for this ward, fifteen minutes for that, five minutes with the matron and an hour with the governors. But Dottie was unable to leave a children's ward in less than half an hour. She started singing a children's song from her own childhood and soon they were all singing it. Every verse ended with a command to start again from the beginning, and it seemed as if they would be there forever. Patients who could walk wandered in to see what the noise was about, and stayed to sing. Young doctors joined in with gusto. One of them winked at Dottie, and she winked back. The song ended only when they were all too weary to go on.

After a while the visits blended seamlessly into each other, the same rides through the streets, the same smiles and cheers. Then there would be dinner with the local dignitaries, during which Dottie could practice being the one to direct the conversation. This was mentally exhausting as it was always up to her to produce new ideas. Luckily Alicia seemed to have relatives wherever they stopped and was a mine of local information. Of course, her secretary would have been even better, but Randolph had contrived to excuse himself on the grounds of pressing work.

After dinner she would sit up with one or two of her ladies, chatting with the top level of her mind, while the rest of it wondered what Randolph was doing at this moment.

One day her driver, confused in a strange place, took a wrong turn and went too far down a narrow street to be able to turn around. Seeking a way out, he drove on and on, until Dottie found herself in a nightmare place.

"It looks as though they've had a fire," she said,

getting out. "At least three streets have gone. But why don't they do something?"

"Because the council's taken all the money," said a surly voice nearby. It belonged to a shabby man who seemed to be living in the ruins of a house.

"Tell me about it," Dottie said at once.

The houses belonged to the local council, and had caught fire years ago. The government had voted money to rebuild but the council bickered endlessly about which department had the right to spend it, while the inhabitants stayed homeless. As the man spoke, more and more people came close and stood listening. Soon there were enough to form a dangerous mob, had they been so inclined. But none of them moved. They were watching Dottie. They knew her face from pictures. Suddenly they had new hope.

By now her official escort had managed to catch up with her, full of profuse apologies, eager to whisk her away, the story half-told. Dottie saw the expressions in the crowd change to cynical. Now she would leave and forget them. She couldn't bear it. Impulsively she spread her hands.

"Don't worry," she told. "I'm going to get this sorted."

There was a sharp intake of breath from close by, but it was drowned by the cheers from the crowd. They believed her.

"Now you've got a tiger by the tail," Alicia observed as they talked that night. "Sternheim is the local 'great man' around her. The ruling clique on the council are mostly his buddies. He protects them and they do as they like."

"Why doesn't the local newspaper make a fuss?"

"He owns it."

It didn't surprise Dottie to find, on arriving home, that Sternheim had been in urgent consultation with Randolph.

"Don't tell me," she said, holding up her hands at the sight of Randolph. "The future queen isn't supposed to make promises, but I've made it now and I have to keep it and that means—"

"Dottie—"

"—that it doesn't matter what Sternheim or anyone else says."

"Dottie—"

"I don't even care what the rules say because—"

"Dottie, will you pipe down and let someone else get a word in edgeways?" he roared.

"Just as long as I've made myself clear."

"Blindingly. Now will you please tell me what happened and how you managed to get Sternheim so rattled."

"He's rattled? Great!" She told him the whole story. "Alicia says he's the local great man. Local pig if you ask me. Anyway, he's got them all by the short and curlies." Randolph winced. "You know what I mean."

"Yes I do, and I beg you not to use that expression to anyone but me."

"Never mind that," she told him impatiently. "Tell me what I can do. What about a decree?"

"No decrees," he said at once. "A decree is a blunt instrument. Save it for a big occasion."

"I only—"

"Button it, and listen. Sternheim will be here in a minute. He'll have heard you're back and he won't waste time."

"Good. I want a word with him."

"No!"

"Yes."

"Dottie, you can't accuse him. It would cause a scandal. He mustn't even suspect that you know of his involvement. There are other ways. I'll talk to him. You don't say a word."

"Oh don't I?" she said, bristling.

"No, because if you do you'll ruin everything, and the people who will suffer will be the ones you've promised to help."

That silenced her, he noticed with a touch of respect. "You leave it to me," he said.

The last words were spoken in a tone that brooked no argument, and for a moment she could see Randolph as the king he should have been. But she couldn't say anything because Sternheim appeared at that moment, bristling with barely suppressed annoyance. But Randolph would put it right, Dottie thought with a surge of confidence.

When the civilities had been gotten out of the way Randolph said, in the smooth voice of a diplomat, "Chancellor, I'm sure you appreciate that our princess is young and unfamiliar with her new duties, and she was wholly unaware of the impropriety of her..."

He managed to make it last for five minutes, during which Dottie stared at him, sick with disillusion. How could he be doing this? Not to her, but to the innocent victims of fire and corruption.

Sternheim was relaxing visibly as the emollient words poured from Randolph. Gradually a smile spread over his smug features.

"I'm sure we can all consider the matter settled," Randolph said at last, "once we've dealt with the small matter of presentation."

"What's that?" Sternheim demanded.

"Her Royal Highness gave a promise in public. People will be watching to see what happens, so we must make it seem as if things are being done. I suggest a commission of inquiry, with full powers to investigate and summon witnesses. They'll speak to the unfortunate residents and everyone on the council, and the accounts department will explain exactly what's happened to the money, and the world will be satisfied."

As he listened to this speech Sternheim's smile had faded and his skin turned an ugly gray. Watching him, Dottie realized that Randolph had pulled a masterstroke. Without uttering a single accusation he'd lured the minister into a trap from which there was only one escape.

"A commission of inquiry," Sternheim said, almost stuttering. "But that'll take time."

"Months," Randolph confirmed. "Since every detail must be uncovered."

"But where are these poor people supposed to live in the meantime?" Sternheim blustered.

"In the ruins, where they're living now," Dottie couldn't resist saying.

"Shocking! Shocking!" Sternheim stammered hastily.

"Your concern does you credit," Randolph told him, "but what else can we do?"

"I know a few people on that council," Sternheim said. "I could put a rocket behind them."

"And get rebuilding started quickly?"

"In a few days. And temporary accommodation for those poor unfortunates in the meantime. Much better than a lengthy commission. Leave it all to me." Sternheim looked at Dottie who was giving him an alarming smile. ''Happy to, er, be of service.''

''I'm sure Her Royal Highness won't object if you left now,'' Randolph said. ''You'll be wanting to get on with things.''

Sternheim mopped his brow and bowed himself out. Randolph turned to Dottie with an air of triumph, and their eyes met. *Yes!*

''You did it,'' she crowed.

''No, we did it,'' he said firmly. ''I did the talking but you provided the substance.''

''Will it work?''

''I think we can look for the bulldozers to start clearing the site double quick, and the building work to proceed soon after. And when things are well under way, and it's too late to stop them—'' he looked at her with almost a touch of mischief.

''What?'' she breathed.

''Then we'll send in the commission.''

Her eyes widened. ''But... Didn't you just make a deal with Sternheim?''

''No, but I let him think I did.''

''Oh, Randolph,'' she breathed in awe, ''you really know how to fight dirty.''

''Thank you, ma'am,'' he said, correctly interpreting this as a compliment. ''I think we've got him by the, er, short and curlies.''

She crowed with laughter, then sobered and admitted, ''You do this better than me.''

''Let's just say we're a good team.''

''The best.''

She moved toward him, her hands outstretched. In another moment she would have thrown her arms about his neck, forgetting everything except that he was wonderful. But then it seemed to her that he flinched and took a half step back. His eyes were fond and smiling, but there was no doubt that he had avoided making contact with her. After their perfect communication it felt like a snub, and her happiness faded.

But not entirely. The moment might have been brief, but it had happened, and she could treasure it.

Even with a kind of truce things were never going to be smooth between them. He was naturally imperious and she was learning fast. Power, Dottie discovered, was the sweetest thing in the world. Better even than ice cream.

Her intervention about the rebuilding had been a triumph. The papers carried the story of, "I'm going to get this sorted," and the sudden activity next day was proof, as though anybody needed it, that Princess Dottie kept her word.

Her success gave her an appetite for more intervention, with varied results. Sometimes she achieved something, more often she misread an unfamiliar situation and put her foot in it. Randolph always managed to smooth things over, but her ministers were beginning to regard her with alarm, and Randolph told her crisply that while she might think of herself as Joan of Arc she actually resembled a loose cannon, blundering across everyone's toes. After that the atmosphere became chilly again.

There was so much to be put right about this country, she decided. Increasing the numbers of female politicians was more complicated than she'd thought. It wasn't just the outdated parliamentary hours, but beyond them a whole raft of laws and social conditions that created pointless obstacles to women.

At least, Dottie thought they were pointless. Enderlin spoke of tradition and the need to move slowly. She spoke of the twenty-first century and the need for Elluria to get there without delay. He clutched his head. She poured him cups of strong tea, which he drank and felt better. He was a courtly, gracious man who never allowed their battles to affect his liking for Dottie, nor allowed that liking to make him yield easily. Soon they could exchange prejudices freely, while staying friends. When things reached crisis point Randolph was called in to referee.

He did so reluctantly. "Can't you cope with her yourself?" he demanded.

"Nobody can cope with her," Enderlin groaned. "Her new idea is to reorganize the civil service training so that everyone can learn to do gardening, which, apparently, is good for the soul."

"She's winding you up," Randolph said, exasperated. "Can't you recognize it yet? If you react she just gets worse."

"I am not used to being 'wound up' by my sovereign," Enderlin replied with dignity. "And I'm too old to start now."

"Nonsense! My father enjoyed practical jokes."

"So he did," Enderlin said, much struck. "I'd forgotten. It's just that from a woman it somehow sounds strange."

"Don't say that to her," Randolph begged in alarm. "She'll give you a speech about equal rights, and this time she *won't* be joking."

"I have to admit that she brightens the place up. I accompanied her on a recent trip to my hometown and she insisted on walking through the streets and talking to the crowd. She noticed a child in a push chair, who'd lost a shoe, and blow me if she didn't pick the shoe up from the pavement and put it on the kiddy's foot herself, then chat to the mother for five minutes about the outrageous price of children's clothes."

"She didn't promise to 'sort' them as well did she?" asked Randolph, alarmed.

"No, I managed to intervene just in time. But, to be fair, it's not anything she says. It's what she is. She gives them that smile...you know the one."

"Yes," Randolph said quietly. "I know the one."

"It seems to bring the sun out for them. Mind you, I'm not sure if that's what a monarch is supposed to do..."

"Could a monarch do better than make the sun shine on her people?" Randolph asked, still in the same quiet voice. "It's a great gift, and she has it."

"Well, I don't deny that she's lovable, and maybe that's important."

Randolph nodded. "And maybe it's the only thing that matters."

"If only somebody could reign her in."

His significant voice and look brought Randolph out of the semitrance in which he'd been wandering. A horrible suspicion of having betrayed himself made him explode, "Forget that idea now and never mention it again."

"But your duty to your country..."

Randolph said something very rude about his duty to his country. Enderlin shook his head, trying to believe he'd really heard what he thought he had, but he couldn't manage it.

"You've never failed in your duty before," he pleaded.

"Ideas of duty vary, Enderlin. I'm doing mine now by trying to teach this crazy woman how to occupy the throne without blowing it up. But I recognize no duty to marry someone who goes through life like a jumping bean. And if my countrymen think otherwise, they are welcome to try it for themselves. Let me make it quite clear to you that she is the last woman I would ever dream of marrying. And that's official."

Then, calming down just a little, he added hurriedly, "But you'll never repeat that to anyone."

Enderlin promised and kept his word. But walls have ears and the story reached Dottie by the end of the day, and duly affected the atmosphere. It was a measure of how far she'd traveled that instead of treating Randolph to her frank opinion of him she merely smiled sweetly at their next meeting, and left him wondering.

Chapter Ten

The first time Dottie saw a picture of Prince Harold she thought there had been a mistake.

"But he's supposed to be a monster. Wow, what a hunk!"

The man in the picture had everything to attract the female fancy, including a brilliant smile, regular features and eyes that seemed to gleam with fun. His mouth was full and sensual, and his body, as another picture revealed, was tall and lean.

"He looks good on horseback," she observed, picking up a third. "You did say that I'd be going riding with him, didn't you?"

"I don't believe your schedule includes it, no," Randolph said coldly.

She looked at him but he didn't return her gaze. His attention was absorbed in some papers and even the set of his shoulders seemed forbidding. She grew cross. Which of them was the boss here?

"Better fix it so that it does," she said coolly.

"That is impossible. The schedule has been laid down and agreed with the Korburg embassy. It cannot be changed now."

"Rubbish, you changed it only yesterday. I know you did."

He still didn't look up but the back of his head clearly revealed his irritation. "And I'm not changing it again," he said through gritted teeth.

"You're not? Don't I get a say?"

"You get too big a say as it is."

"My people have no complaints. Ask them."

"Oh yes, I've seen the latest opinion polls. They see you visiting sick children and homeless shelters, and they adore you because you do it wonderfully well."

"That's not all I do."

"No, some of your meddling has been lucky."

"Meddling? How dare you!"

"What about the mayor of Sellingen?"

"I apologized for that."

"And the wretched little man whom you decided was running a disorderly house?"

"It was a misunderstanding. He forgave me. Those roses over there come from his garden."

Yes, that was it, Randolph thought, exasperated. She made the most outrageous mistakes, brought them all to the edge of disaster and her victims sent her roses.

"You jump in with both feet, never stopping to ask questions first, and count on people only remembering your successes," he said. "There are rules that govern these things, just as there are rules that govern every aspect of your life now. The sooner you get used to that the better."

"Oh, I know about the rules. It doesn't mean I'm going to lie down under every single one. Maybe I can change some of them."

"Then you will do it after due consultation with me," he said bluntly. "And don't threaten me with a decree or any of that nonsense."

"I've never actually issued one yet, just talked about it."

"Yes, because you rely on the threat to bring people to heel. I give you credit for trying. But often you're not trying in the right way."

"You mean I'm not doing it your way. But why should I?"

"Because I happen to know a great deal more about what this country needs than someone who's still playing games."

"If that's what you think I wonder you tolerate me here at all. Send me back and have Harold. I'm sure he knows what he's doing."

She could have bitten her tongue off as soon as the words were out. Randolph's eyes grew cold with contempt.

"I thought better of you than that. Blackmail. Cheap, and despicable."

She knew it and would have given anything to unsay the words. But she couldn't admit it to the bitterly contemptuous man who turned his scorn on her now.

"You're playing at being queen, Dottie. No more than that. Don't turn away from me." He seized her arm as she turned and pulled her unceremoniously back to face him.

"Let me go," she snapped.

"Not till you've heard me out."

"Let me go at once, or I'll scream and bring the guards in."

"I'm trembling."

"You should. 'Laying unauthorized hands' on the monarch is high treason. You taught me that."

"Why, you cheeky little—"

"Calling the monarch names is probably treason, too. I'm sure I could find a law about it somewhere. But I won't need to. You won't risk me calling the guards. Think how undignified it would be."

In the silence his hand fell from her arm. Nothing in his lifelong training had prepared him for this situation, and his outrage and confusion were almost tangible.

Dottie took advantage of it to say, "You have our permission to leave."

"What?"

"The crown princess gives you her permission to leave."

"Dottie, you're beginning to do it very well but—"

"You will address me as Your Royal Highness, and you will not approach me again until I say so."

She was shocked by her own temerity. After a stunned moment Randolph stepped away, bowed his head, clicked his heels and departed without a backward glance.

Everybody knew. In less than an hour the news of the breach had gone through the palace. By the next day everyone knew that it was worse than that. Prince Randolph had waited one day to give her the chance to summon him. When she didn't, he'd taken off to his estate in a terrible rage.

"He was just like this as a boy," Aunt Liz recalled. "There were dreadful storms, when it was best to keep out of his way. But don't worry. Just give him a little time to calm down, then send for him again."

"In a pig's eye I'll send for him."

"Then you seem condemned to perpetual stalemate," Aunt Liz said crossly.

"No way. He'll bring me the papers tomorrow as usual, and I'll let him know that he's forgiven."

"For what?"

"For incurring my royal displeasure," Dottie said with a chuckle.

There was something to be said for being royal. You could win every argument.

But next morning there was no sign of Randolph. His assistant appeared with a message to say that he'd been called away unexpectedly to settle a matter of administration in the princess's service. He would deal with it speedily, and on his return would give himself the honor of reporting to her, etcetera. Dottie made a suitable response, and wished she could have Randolph there for just five minutes, to tell him what she thought of him.

He was gone four days, then five, then a week. Dottie, who'd prepared a dignified speech, grew infuriated at never being able to deliver it.

When he did return after a week, and a servant came to say that he would wait upon her, she was so annoyed that she sent a message to say that she would inform him when it was convenient for her to see him.

After that there was silence.

"Why doesn't he report to me?" she demanded of Aunt Liz.

"Because you told him not to. Do you think a man of Randolph's pride is going to risk another snub?"

"Okay, so he can just sit there and sulk."

"Yes, and you can sit here and sulk. And that'll make two of you sulking while the country goes to rack and ruin. I've no patience with either of you. Call him up and tell him how much you've missed him."

"No way."

"Dottie, why ever not?"

"Because I'm the crown princess," she said miserably.

Somehow being royal was no guard against feeling that the world was empty because one man wasn't there. There had been nothing between them but kisses, anger and the half-admitted flaring of desire, but now she longed for more. Kisses weren't enough. She ached for him.

She wanted to know if his body, beneath his clothes, was as hard and athletic as she suspected. She'd had so little opportunity to find out, and the thought tormented her night and day. She wanted him to kiss her deeply, powerfully, and then do more than kiss her. She wanted him to take her wherever passion could lead them. She wanted him to show her the whole world.

But he wasn't there.

As Harold's visit neared, there was a series of meetings between politicians and civil servants, which Dottie insisted on attending. She wanted to know every detail of the arrangements. There were receptions, a state banquet and a ball in Harold's honor. There would be a performance at the State Opera House, and Harold would be asked to give a speech to parliament. So far so good.

But Harold also wanted to visit Korenhausen, a magnificent country mansion, where his grandmother had been born.

"He couldn't stand the old lady," Sternheim snapped. "What's he playing at?"

"I suppose he wants to stand there looking 'deeply affected' for the sake of the photographers," Durmand said. "And to remind everyone that he has Ellurian royal blood."

"So have I, and I come from an older line, which is why I'm here and he isn't," said Dottie, who'd been studying hard. "Let him do what he wants. Is there anything else?"

"Just one thing ma'am," Durmand said. "It'll be hard to—"

"What is it?" Dottie asked. Not only had Durmand stopped but his eyes, and those of every other man in the room, were riveted on the door. Turning, she saw Randolph standing there with a brow like thunder.

"Out, all of you," he said curtly.

His manner was so grim and purposeful that every man around the table forgot that Randolph was officially a nobody, and rose to leave the room. Dottie rose too, to confront him indignantly. But instead of being impressed by his sovereign's wrath he took firm hold of her arm.

"I didn't tell you to leave," he said.

"What?"

"I said stay here."

The door closed behind the last man.

"And just what do you think you're doing?" she demanded.

"I came to commit high treason," he said, pulling her into his arms and silencing her mouth with his own.

The sudden granting of what she'd yearned for was a stunning shock, obliterating everything except sensation. It was glorious to have his lips against her own again, thrilling to feel the implicit promise in his movements, and despite her indignation she felt herself yielding to temptation.

But then, having let her glimpse wonders, he slammed the door again, drawing back a few inches, but keeping hold of her shoulders.

"Don't you ever keep me out again," he growled.

Her temper flared. "And don't you tell me what to do. I'm the queen."

"Not until your coronation, and not if I wring your neck first."

"As if!" she scoffed.

He was holding her just far enough away so that she could see his intense, blazing eyes. This wasn't the Randolph she knew, the urbane, worldly wise aristocrat, or the friend and mentor whose exasperation with her was usually tinged with wry amusement. This was a man driven beyond endurance, no longer in command of himself. Something stirred in her—not quite alarm, but certainly a feeling of danger. She realized suddenly how helpless she was, alone with him, now that he was too angry to be careful. She hadn't known that danger could be so thrilling.

"I have spent the last two days twiddling my thumbs, waiting for *Your Royal Highness* to deign to remember my existence." Randolph said the words with savage emphasis. "Do you really think you can treat me like that and get away with it? Because if so, you're living in cloud-cuckoo-land."

"Is this the man who told me to remember my royal dignity?"

"Not with me—"

"Yes, even with you."

"Careful Dottie. You're letting power go to your head."

"That's what it's for!" she yelled.

"You have so much to learn. Don't ever insult me like that again, because I promise you I won't be a gentleman about it."

"Is this you being a gentleman?"

"This is me letting you know what I will and will not put up with, and what I will *not* put up with is being ignored by you while the entire court sniggers at me. Do you understand?"

"I would have seen you any time the week before, but you weren't there," she cried. "You were sulking at your estate."

"I do not sulk."

"Well, it sure looked like it to me."

His eyes glinted. He'd spent the past few weeks learning deference to this maddening woman, but the lessons had come very hard to him. Suddenly it all fell away and he was once more *Prince* Randolph, reared to pride and arrogance from the day of his birth. "I don't let anyone talk to me like that," he said softly.

"I just did."

"And you won't do so again. Not if you know what's good for you."

She grew lofty. "Have you forgotten who you're talking to?"

"*I* haven't forgotten, but I think *you* have—Dottie Hebden, who used to be charming but has gotten much too big for her boots."

"No, I'm just wearing bigger boots. Why should you complain? You put them on me. I'm not 'little Dottie Hebden' anymore, Randolph. She vanished. If you don't like the new me, tough. You created me. I'm Crown Princess Dorothea, soon to be Queen Dorothea III, and you could get a life sentence for assaulting my royal person!"

"Then I may as well be hung for a sheep as a lamb," he muttered, tightening his grip.

"How dare you—"

"Shut up." He covered her mouth again.

This time there was no doubt that her royal person was being assaulted. He was doing what he wanted, and to hell with her objections! She should have been full of righteous indignation at this disrespect, but she wasn't. She didn't want respect. She wanted excitement. She wanted to be made aware of her own body as never before. She wanted what he was doing now, forcing her to recognize him as a man responding to her as a woman.

It was the first unambiguous proof she'd had that he desired her as much as she desired him, and she rejoiced in it. He wasn't faking the fierce movements of his lips, and the knowledge went through and through her with thrills of pleasure that seemed to be everywhere at once.

He wore no jacket, and through the thin material of his shirt she could feel his heated body, hard as a rock. There was no way she could have struggled against the strength in his arms, even if she'd wanted to. There was more than desire in this. He was showing her where the power really lay, so that she wouldn't kid herself about it. But there were other ways to demonstrate power. He'd chosen this one because he wanted her as much as she did him, on a basic level that had nothing to do with their fights. And he, too, was kidding himself if he thought he could kiss her like this and forget about it. There was no going back now.

Randolph couldn't have defined what had overtaken him, except that it had been a long time coming. He'd taken other orders from her and learned to grin and bear it. But no more!

"You can keep anyone else out," he growled. "But not me."

"You won't get in here another time," she murmured, deliberately provoking him.

"I'll get in no matter how many doors I have to break down. Why don't you call your guards and have me arrested?"

"For what?" she whispered.

"For this," he said tightening his arms again and kissing her lightly, swiftly, caressing her face with his lips while he murmured to her, "You're a fool, Dottie—but I'm a fool, too...."

His tongue was flickering against her lips, until she let them fall open. She was winning. At any moment—

And then she felt him stiffen, heard the swift muttered curse as he drew away from her, and her hopes came crashing down.

The door had opened, and all the men who had so spinelessly abandoned her to this predator were creeping sheepishly back, having belatedly remembered which one of them was the monarch. Now they looked distinctly nervous at the prospect of challenging Randolph.

"It's all right," he said. "I'd finished." He released Dottie abruptly. His face was pale and his chest was still rising and falling, but he'd regained control of himself. As he made his way to the door, there was a touch of nonchalance in his manner.

"You can get on with your meeting now," he said.

And he walked out.

Korburg was a small state just over the border, and unlike Elluria it was not a kingdom, only a principality. As such, it was a "poor relation" and not strictly entitled to the full panoply of honors for a state visit. But Dottie insisted on them. She had a point to make.

On the day of Harold's arrival she was waiting on the carpeted platform as his train glided in, to the accompaniment of the Korburg national anthem. The double doors of the special train slid open, and a man stepped out who was everything his picture had suggested, and more.

Dottie advanced the length of the red carpet to greet him. Flashbulbs went off as the press recorded their meeting. He took her hand in both of his and gave her a big, charming smile. For a brief moment she was overwhelmed by this dazzling, attractive man.

But the moment passed. Dottie hadn't been a waitress and a barmaid without learning how to read men's smiles. The mouth stretched but the eyes calculated. Will she, won't she? Fair game, anyway. Despite his splendid looks there was something disagreeable about him.

I'd enjoy slapping your face, my lad, she thought.

But for the moment she had to defer that pleasure, and greet him with the appearance of friendliness. Then they must sit side by side in the open carriage, drawn by four white horses, and parade through the streets of Wolfenberg while crowds waved and cheered.

"Already you have won your people's hearts," Harold said. "I congratulate you on your success."

She responded appropriately, but she wasn't fooled. He was here to look her over and if he could find any sign of weakness he would pounce. But Dottie was equally determined that he would find nothing.

He was there for three packed days. That night there was a state banquet at which they sat side by side through six courses and ten speeches. They toasted each other. He smiled. She smiled. Randolph did not smile.

Harold paid a sentimental visit to Korenhausen, where he made a short, touching speech. He addressed parliament, with Dottie sitting in the gallery to lead the applause. They didn't ride together because, despite her command, Randolph had mysteriously forgotten to include it in the itinerary. But Harold was her host at a banquet at the Korburg embassy. She was his hostess for a performance of *The Marriage of Figaro* by the Ellurian State Opera. Dottie had gone glassy-eyed at this prospect, having never seen an opera before, but knowing it was bound to be boring. But halfway through the overture she found herself tapping her foot in time to the music, and after that everything was fine.

Harold was charm itself, playing the gallant to Dottie, and kissing her hand at every opportunity until she wished he would stop. He had a big, apparently genial smile which he turned on everyone, but above it his eyes were calculating and he missed nothing. Most of all, he saw that she was popular.

On his last evening there was a ball at the palace. They led the dance while the onlookers applauded.

"I've been eager for this moment," he said.

"But of course. We are both heads of state. It's only proper that we dance together first."

"That's not what I mean, and I think you know it. You're a beautiful woman, and now I have my arms around you, where they belong."

"You're too kind," she murmured. "Of course, I know that your position obliges you to pay me compliments, prince."

"To hell with my position. You inflame me to madness."

Dottie fought down a desire to laugh. Was she supposed to take this stuff seriously?

"I underestimated you," Harold went on, visibly preening himself. "Now that I know you better I believe we can do business."

"Business?" she considered the word. "You mean the kind of business you've been doing with those international companies who want to get at Elluria's minerals?"

"I? How could I do that? The minerals are yours to sell, not mine."

"That's right. So it isn't true?"

"True?"

"That you've been accepting money on the promise of concessions to be delivered when you take over as king of Elluria?''

His face became gray with temper, but Dottie's sunny gaze at him never wavered, and after a moment he laughed.

''Of course it's not true.''

''And it's not true either that certain people are pressing you to cough up or repay the money?''

''Pardon? Cough up?''

''Never mind. I'm sure it's a terrible slander.''

''You know how rumors get around. That wasn't the kind of business I had in mind.'' He tightened his arm about her waist.

''Prince, please,'' she murmured modestly. ''We are observed. People will talk.''

''Underlings. What do their opinions matter? I wish I could make you realize what this visit has meant to me. I'm thinking and feeling so many strange, unexpected things. Do you understand me?''

Perfectly, she thought with grim humor. *I know your kind. Flash Harry! All teeth and trousers!*

But she met his gaze, wide-eyed, and shook her head.

''I thought you wouldn't. You're so new at this game, that's what's enchanting about you.''

She nodded. ''Everyone finds me enchanting since I became a crown princess,'' she confided innocently.

That threw him because he wasn't sure how serious she was. He gave an uncertain smile, wondering if she was daring to make fun of him. Dottie's answering gaze was as guileless as a baby's, and she saw him relax, reassured that she really was as stupid as she'd allowed herself to seem.

"We can't talk now," she murmured, "but later perhaps...on the terrace?"

The music ended. She gave him a dazzling smile and departed for her next dance. For an hour she passed from one distinguished nonentity to the next, making conversation with the top layer of her mind, while the rest noticed when Sophie danced with Harold and when with Randolph.

At last she had a moment to sit down. She leaned toward Jeanie, who was in attendance on her that night. "Ask Prince Randolph if he would like the honor of dancing with me," she commanded regally. She then spoilt the effect by adding, "And tell him he'd better, or else."

A moment later Randolph appeared. "I am bowed down by the honor," he said as he extended his arm.

"I'll stamp on your toes if you talk to me like that," she threatened.

"I see that we still understand each other," he said ironically.

Being in Randolph's arms was nothing like being in Harold's. One man was full of lush compliments, overpoweringly attentive. The other was like a hedgehog. Yet with Harold she'd thought constantly of the moment of escape. With Randolph she thought only of Randolph, of how it would be if he held her close, so that she could feel his body move against her own.

The last time he'd held her was the day he'd stormed into the meeting, when he'd abandoned all control. But now his control was perfect again, and he danced as he did everything, correctly.

"How am I doing for my first state visit?" she asked.

"You're overdoing it," he replied coolly.

"Is that all you've got to say? And I was trying so hard to please you."

"What does it have to do with me?"

"Well, you're my mentor. Practically my father figure." The sudden tightening of his hand in the small of her back was almost imperceptible, but she felt it nonetheless, and it eased her heart. She turned the screw a little. "I rely on your fatherly advice."

"You wouldn't take any advice I could give you Dottie, and if you think I'm going to help you play off your tricks, you're mistaken."

"I don't know what you mean."

"You know exactly what I mean. There's a very shrewd brain underneath that blond fluff. And don't look at me like that either."

"Like what?"

"Bland and innocent."

She laughed. "Perhaps I really am bland and innocent."

"Not you. You're a witch. Dottie, stop it! I told you not to look at me like that."

Her laughter rang out. "Just ignore me. It's easy."

He eyed her with grim appreciation of these tactics. "Be careful," he said softly. "Harold is a dangerous man. If you're doing what I think you are, let me warn you, your people won't stand for it."

"Randolph, you have absolutely no idea what I'm doing, so don't kid yourself."

And he really didn't know, she thought. He was that blind. In fact, he was probably so blind that he wouldn't notice when she slipped away onto the terrace with Harold.

The moment came an hour later, when everyone was being refreshed with champagne. In honor of her distinguished guest Dottie carried two glasses out herself and they sat side by side to toast each other.

"To you, Dottie," he said. "You don't mind if I call you that?"

"No, I still answer to it, with my friends." She didn't say whether he was one of them.

"You've come a long way."

"And I'll bet you know just how far."

"It wasn't easy, but my researchers managed to track down The Grand Hotel. Manageress, eh?"

"Haven't your researchers found out any more?"

"Oh yes. I know you were nothing but a glorified barmaid. Who cares? You are a shrewd, ambitious woman, and I think we understand each other."

"You keep my secret and I keep yours?" she asked archly.

"Precisely. And the best way for us to do that is—" abruptly he pulled her into his arms.

She had to fight not to gag. He was disgusting. She made a movement to box his ears, but stopped herself in time. Don't spoil it now, she thought. She laid her hands gently on his shoulders, as though she was willing but restrained by modesty.

They were like that when Randolph came to find Dottie.

Nothing could have gone better, she thought, lying in bed that night, looking into the darkness. Harold had been nonchalant, the very picture of a ladies' man caught in the act and loving it. Randolph had been furious and unable to say so, although there had been a look of angry reproach in his eyes that thrilled and hurt her at the same time.

She stretched and was about to settle down to sleep when she heard a noise at the French doors that led onto the balcony. She sat up and it came again, the soft movement of the latch, and then the sound of the door being opened, and somebody slipping quietly in.

"What are you doing here?" she cried.

"Sssh!" Harold said urgently, hurrying across the room to the bed. As he reached one side she slid out of the other.

"Keep away from me," she said, feeling around for her robe without taking her eyes from him. Too late she realized that the robe was close to Harold.

He followed her eyes and whisked it up.

"Can I have that please?"

"Of course." He began to move forward.

"Just throw it to me, and get right out."

"You want me to walk out of that door?" he said indicating the door to the outer chamber.

Dottie froze. Out there was a lady-in-waiting, on night duty, and in the corridor outside were two footmen. No way could they be allowed to see Harold leaving her bedroom.

"Leave the way you arrived," she insisted. "Come to think of it, how did you arrive?"

"You don't pay your maid enough."

"You bribed her?"

"It's the simplest way. I got here before you, using the rear corridors. She let me in, I went out to wait on the balcony and she left the windows unlocked, I just crouched down behind the parapet. I thought we could talk better like this."

"I have nothing to say to you."

"I think you have. You like being crown princess,

I've seen it. As my consort, you'll still enjoy all the goodies. We'll both gain."

"Marry you?" she said in a voice of pure scorn. "You're the last man I'd ever marry."

"My dear, I'm the last man you'll have the chance to marry. Soon everyone will know that I'm here. You'll have no choice. But let's make quite sure, shall we?"

He moved fast but Dottie was faster, slicing her hand across his nose in a swift movement that made him squeal like a pig.

"Right," he said, speaking rather nasally, "if that's how you want it I'm happy to oblige."

Ducking her second blow he grasped her shoulders and pulled her hard against him. At such close range she couldn't fight effectively, and it seemed that nothing could stop him lowering his mouth to hers. He was getting nearer…

"Leave her alone." It was Randolph's voice that cracked like a whip from the shadows.

He stepped forward into the light, his face livid. Behind him Dottie could see four other men.

Time stopped. Dottie freed herself from Harold's frozen hands and stepped back. Cornered, Harold stared around at them all with loathing.

"You're fools, all of you," he raged. "You give your loyalty to that?" He pointed at Dottie. "That? A queen? She's a barmaid, that's all. A cheap, jumped-up little barmaid, giving herself airs. And you fell for it."

Randolph started forward with murder in his eyes, but Dottie moved first.

Her knee came up sharp, hard and aimed with deadly accuracy. Harold fell onto the bed, clutching himself and moaning, while she regarded him with satisfaction.

"I wasn't a barmaid for nothing," she observed.

A cheer went up from her defenders. They laughed and applauded while Dottie clapped a hand over her mouth in horror.

"I shouldn't have said that," she squealed, looking in horror at Randolph.

But he too was laughing. "We are all your friends here," he said. "And we're all proud of you."

As if to prove it the men applauded some more. Looking around she recognized them all as soldiers who'd been her escorts at various times.

"They volunteered," Randolph told her, reading her expression. "Your whole army is loyal to you, but these are 'your' men in a special way." As he spoke he was slipping a robe over her disheveled nightgown.

"How did you all come to be here?" she asked.

"Bertha is more loyal than she seemed. Having pocketed Harold's bribe she came straight to me. I told her not to breathe a word to you, and when you'd gone to bed she let us all in. You were never in any real danger."

"Thank you so much, all of you," she said, spreading her arms wide to the soldiers.

"Don't think you really needed us though," one of them said, provoking a laugh.

Harold was still writhing and choking. Two of them raised him to his feet and would have removed him, but Randolph stopped them.

"My dear cousin," he said tenderly to Harold, "don't go without being the first to congratulate us. Princess Dorothea has honored me by agreeing to become my wife.'' He turned swiftly to Dottie. ''I know you'll forgive me for announcing it like this, but there are reasons why Harold should be the first to know.''

The soldiers were in ecstasies. Dottie regarded Randolph with a fulminating eye, but there was nothing she could say in front of an audience.

What had she expected? Moonlight on a rose-strewn balcony? A tender declaration? This was a marriage of state. Yet his kisses had surely told her of something more, and she felt a quickening of excitement, even through her indignation at his high-handed behavior.

At last they were alone, and she confronted Randolph.

'''First to know' is right,'' she seethed. ''Harold knew before I did.''

''Nonsense Dottie, you've always known that our marriage was inevitable. You promised to do whatever your country needed. Now you know what it needs, and quickly. We can't take chances. He'll try something else, and we have to spike his guns.''

''Of course,'' she said in a colorless voice.

That was how he saw their marriage, she realized—spiking Harold's guns.

Chapter Eleven

Elluria had never known such celebrations. Two royal weddings, one after another. First Prince Harold of Korburg would marry Sophie Bekendorf in Wolfenberg Cathedral, and the very next day their own Princess Dorothea would be united in wedlock to Prince Randolph. A few weeks after that there would be the coronation. The makers of royal souvenirs were working overtime turning out mugs, tea towels and anything else that they could think of.

Much as she disliked Sophie, Dottie felt sorry for her as she flaunted Harold's huge engagement ring, and boasted of his passionate proposal. Did she know, Dottie wondered, that her future husband was saving face, having failed to seduce Elluria's future queen?

The only story that came out of that night's events was her own betrothal. Randolph had scotched the scandal very effectively. Dottie only wished she knew what other motives he might have had.

These days every spare moment was taken up with preparations for their wedding, and they hardly saw each other except in public. She kept promising herself that she would talk to him privately, but what was there to say? This was a state marriage, and all the talking in the world wouldn't change it.

When they'd discussed a honeymoon he'd suggested Venice, Rome, New York and several other glamorous places. But Dottie had turned them down.

"Too public," she said. "I'd rather go somewhere quiet in Elluria."

Several of his friends offered her the use of their country houses, but Dottie claimed that all of them were too large, too palatial.

At last Randolph said hesitantly, "There's my own estate of Kellensee, but it's little more than a farm."

"Then it'll suit me better than a palace," Dottie said at once.

If he noticed that after raising difficulties about the others she fell in with this suggestion at once, he never said so. A message was sent that night, ordering Kellensee to be prepared.

The question of who was to give her away had caused a few headaches. As she had no close male relatives it was the prerogative of the chancellor, Sternheim. Dottie had groaned and prepared to dig her heels in, but then she'd noticed Sternheim looking at her like a dog expecting to be kicked, and realized that he was terrified of a public rebuff.

Her reaction was to advance on him with hands outstretched, smiling as she said, "Shall we call a truce? You can hardly give me away if we're not speaking, can you?''

Stripped of his usual self-possession, Sternheim stammered out something about being honored, glared furiously at everyone around him and hurried away. The last citadel had fallen to her. Durmand, watching from the sidelines, murmured, ''That's a very clever lady.''

''No,'' Randolph said quietly. ''That's a very kind lady.''

But Dottie heard none of this.

On the day of the first wedding Randolph and Dottie drove together through the streets of Wolfenberg to the cathedral. Soon Harold arrived and took his place before the altar, waiting for his bride.

Dottie had to admit that Sophie was magnificent as she walked down the aisle on her father's arm, her long train streaming behind her. She wondered if Randolph was thinking that this was the day Sophie should have become his wife, but when she stole a glance at him he was brushing something from his sleeve.

It was much worse at the wedding reception when protocol obliged her to dance with Harold while Randolph danced with the bride. Dottie refused to look their way even once, but she couldn't stop her thoughts following them jealously around the floor.

And then the next day it was all to do again, except that this time she was the bride, despairingly conscious that a person of only five foot one could never match Sophie in splendor.

Her snowy dress was lace, specially woven by Elluria's famous lace makers. Her veil was held by a pearl tiara, part of the crown jewels. More pearls hung about her neck and from her ears. Queen Dorothea II had worn these same jewels to her wedding in 1874. Now they adorned Queen Dorothea III, as she would be known after her coronation.

Sounds below told her that Randolph was leaving for the cathedral. She would have stolen a glimpse but a shocked Aunt Liz barred her way to the balcony, uttering dire warnings about "bad luck."

A message from the stables gave her details of the horses that would draw her carriage, led by Jack, the oldest animal in service and coming to the end of his working life. To be drawn by Jack was a promise of good luck.

And she was going to need good luck, she thought. She'd taken a huge gamble to marry the man she loved, uncertain of his true feelings for her. And perhaps she would never truly know. That was the real gamble.

But she would take it and risk the consequences. What was life if you were afraid to seize your chances?

Her procession was a long one. As she stepped outside to be handed into her carriage by Sternheim, proud to bursting point, the leading horsemen were already turning out of the main gates. They were followed by two open carriages containing the six bridesmaids, then a division of the royal cavalry and finally the bridal carriage, escorted by outriders.

And all this was for her, little Dottie Hebden, from Wenford.

She never forgot that drive to the cathedral. She'd known her people had accepted her more readily than she'd dared to hope, but now, as she went through streets lined with cheering crowds, smiling, wishing her well, she understood how completely they'd taken her to their hearts. She'd come home. She was eager to accept this place as home, as hers. She could embrace them, as they had embraced her.

She thought of Randolph and the embrace they would share that night. And then surely she could win his heart as he had won hers? She would banish his last regret about Sophie. At that moment she came within the sound of the cathedral bells, greeting her with a wild, joyous clamor, and she smiled in response. Her heart was high and her courage was enough to dare anything.

In a few minutes they drew up outside the cathedral. Her bridesmaids were waiting to assist her with her train and the long veil, and then they were all ready for the walk down the aisle.

The cathedral was large enough to seat over two thousand, but Dottie saw only one man as she moved along the red carpet that led to the altar. Randolph stood, tall and proud, his face turned in her direction. He didn't smile. If anything, his face was rather stern, and gave no clue to his thoughts. Perhaps he saw her, or perhaps he saw another woman, the one he'd really wanted.

Seeing him from a distance she understood that he was imposing, not because of his rank but because of himself. Even without a title he would always draw the attention of men and women, especially women. It wasn't merely his fine looks, the handsome set of his head and his dark, expressive eyes that would attract them. They would look at him with calculating eyes, reading the promise of pleasure in those long limbs and hard, narrow hips. They would understand the power, no less fierce for being concealed by his formal clothes, and also by the innate restraint of his nature.

She herself didn't fully understand that power, but she suspected it, and the suspicion gave an edge to every thought, every feeling and sensation. As she stepped forward to stand by his side she had never felt more alive.

The ceremony was long and impressive, but it reached her from a distance. All that she was really aware of was Randolph stepping forward, his face paler than she'd ever seen it. He took her hand and for a moment she thought that his was shaking. But she must have imagined that.

In ancient, traditional words they took each other as man and wife. At last the priest smiled, looking from one to the other.

"You may kiss the bride," he said.

Strangely, this was the moment for which she'd been nervous, for she still didn't know on which ground this marriage stood. But when Randolph lifted her veil it was as though the white gauze shut out the world, leaving only themselves. His eyes were kind, full of a question, and she understood, with astonishment, that he was as uncertain as herself.

His lips lay gently on hers for only a moment, but as he drew back they shared a smile that the congregation, murmuring with pleasure, couldn't see.

The organ burst into joy overhead as they turned to go back down the aisle, united.

As they stepped out into the sunlight the crowd cheered their relief. Now they really felt safe from Harold.

The cheering became deafening when Dottie tossed her bouquet high into the air, to go sailing over the crowd and land in a confusion of excited squeals. It was something royal brides never did, but she did it anyway.

As they drove back to the palace she thought ahead to the reception. So many long speeches, so much protocol, so many hours before she could be alone with him. After weeks of fencing she would find out what kind of man Randolph really was. What would she find? Would she be glad or sorry?

The reception moved too slowly for her. At last came the moment she had looked forward to, when her groom led her onto the floor and took her in his arms for the first waltz. They had danced before, but not like this. Now they were husband and wife.

"Are you sorry?" he asked, oddly grave for a bridegroom.

"Should I be? Only you know the answer."

"Trust me, Dottie," he said abruptly, as though she'd touched a nerve.

"I have another wedding present for you. I was saving it for later, but I want to tell you now. I've signed the letters patent."

"You've what?"

"The ones that make you officially Prince Consort. I didn't like leaving it up in the air."

She thought he would react. After all, this last step was the one he'd really wanted, but he only looked at her with an odd little smile.

"Randolph?"

"I'm sorry. I was thinking how lovely you look."

"Did you hear what I said?"

"Yes. Thank you. When can we escape and leave them all behind?"

"I don't think they'd mind if we went soon."

There were grins and kindly laughter when the bride slipped away to change. Their entourage, which had gone on ahead, was minuscule by Dottie's usual standards; just Bertha, being rewarded for dealing cleverly with Harold, and a valet. Randolph drove the car himself.

It was dark when they reached Kellensee and she formed only a brief impression of the building, solid and comfortable, but not palatially huge. To please the servants they sat down to a small meal and toasted each other in champagne, but at last the servants melted away, and Randolph said, "Come with me."

Taking her hand he led her, not upstairs, but to a room at the back of the house. It was an oak paneled room, dominated by a large bed, with a few small rugs on the floor and the bare necessities of furniture.

"Not what you expected?" Randolph asked, a little wryly.

"I love it. It's cozy and friendly. Just like a real home."

She knew she'd said the right thing. His face broke into a smile of real warmth. "If you feel that, then all is well."

"Wasn't it well before?"

He took her face between his hands. "Things will always be well between us, Dottie, I promise you."

"You can't," she whispered longingly. "Nobody can promise that."

"I know that there's been much between us that has been difficult. So many quarrels, so many times when we couldn't be completely honest with each other, so much anger and mistrust. But those things have no place here, now. Let there be just us, and as long as we live, I'll never give you cause to regret that you married me."

"I shall start regretting it soon if you don't kiss me."

He paused just a moment, searching her face for something that he might or might not have found there, she couldn't tell. Then his mouth touched hers and all thought stopped.

Throughout their short engagement he'd maintained a correct distance, so that this was their first kiss since the day he'd burst in on her. That had been an assertion of power, and it was a million miles away from the gentle coaxing she felt in his lips now. She let her mouth fall open, inviting him, eager for the feel of his tongue, relishing its purposeful movements against the soft inside of her cheek, feeling her whole body turned to molten liquid.

His kisses changed, became more demanding and her blood leapt in response. She began to explore his mouth as he had explored hers. She was filled with urgency. With every inch of her she wanted what came next, and when she felt his fingers at the fastening of her dress she moved quickly to help him. When it had slipped to the floor he dropped his lips to the hollow of her neck, teasing her with such skill that she felt the beginnings of a slow burning fire deep inside her. Its soft intensity seemed to possess her so completely that she noticed only vaguely that he was removing the rest of her clothes.

He threw aside his shirt and drew her against him gently, so that the hair on his chest rasped slightly against her breasts. She put her arms around his neck in a gesture of abandon that seemed natural now.

She felt his hands at her waist, lifting her off her

feet and raising her so that the distance in height between them was canceled, and it was she who looked down on him. She took his face between her hands and rained kisses on it, willing him not to delay any more. Her excitement was growing by the minute.

She didn't know when he'd moved to the bed, only that they were suddenly there and he was lowering her, tearing off the rest of his clothes, then lying beside her.

Her caressed her everywhere with his hands, his lips, until the sweet torment grew almost unbearable. She wanted to urge him on, yet at the same time she was content to leave this to him, because only an expert could bring those sensations into magical being.

She thought she knew her own body, but now she realized they'd been only casually acquainted. It had been something to be scrubbed down in the bath and toweled quickly to keep warm. Randolph was intent on revealing her to herself, a desirable woman, all the more desirable because of her response to his maleness.

There was a whole world between men and women that had been hidden from her. As she discovered it now she wondered how she'd lived so long in ignorance. Because he hadn't been there was the answer.

He slipped his knee between her legs, which parted for him easily so that he could move over her. The feel of him coming into her was almost shocking in its beauty and she drew a long breath, willing it to go on and on. This was the meaning of the obscure yearnings that had troubled her. All this time she'd wanted Randolph inside her, and nothing else would do. Now that she'd experienced him, she wondered how she'd endured the wait.

She moved back against him, claiming, releasing, instinctively in harmony. As if by a signal he tossed aside the last of restraint and drove into her vigorously and she cried out with the sharpness of her pleasure. And after that it grew stronger until it enveloped her completely and there was nothing left of her, except that she was reborn and found herself back in his arms, where she had always belonged.

Dottie awoke first and sat up gently so as not to disturb Randolph. That wasn't easy as his big body was sprawled all over the bed. In the night she'd discovered the true Randolph, not the disciplined person of the daylight, but some other man who could abandon himself heart and soul. He'd held nothing back, pleasing her and showing her how to please him, until they were both drained.

Just for now she wanted solitude, to come to terms with the new person she'd become, so she eased herself gently out of bed and looked around for her clothes. There was her dress, just as he'd removed it and tossed it away, too urgent in his desire for her to care if it was ruined. And it was ruined, she saw, noticing a small rent with delight. As she drew the dress against her body every silken movement felt like a caress, bringing memories flooding back. She smiled blissfully…

As he was still sleeping, she found her nightdress, pulled a robe over it and opened the French doors.

They led straight out into the garden, and now that it was daylight she saw for the first time how small a place this was. Not to her. After Wenford everywhere looked spacious, but to a man raised in palaces this was tiny. Yet it was his retreat, his refuge.

The house might have belonged to any solidly prosperous country gentleman. Outside was a small park with a pond on which ducks glided contentedly. She went down to the edge and at once they swam toward her, then away again, quacking with disgust because she was empty handed. She laughed and turned back to the house to find Randolph watching her. He opened his arms and she ran into them.

For a moment they held each other close, in silence. There was nothing to say. What had happened last night was too deep for words.

"I was afraid you wouldn't like this place," he said after a long time.

"I love it. I want to stay here forever. If only we could."

"If only." He kissed her lightly. "Let me show you my home, and make it your home, too."

Over breakfast he told her to wear casual clothes, which would once have been easy, but nothing in Dottie's wardrobe was really casual now. She compromised with a silk shirt and a pair of elegant tweed pants, but Randolph was in the authentic gear, shabby jeans and an old sweatshirt. After one look Dottie burst out laughing.

"I never wear anything else while I'm here," he said.

Kellensee was a working farm, just large enough to be self-supporting. Randolph raised cattle and sheep, and although he had a manager it was clear he was closely involved.

"It belonged to my father," he said as they wandered hand in hand through meadows filled with wild flowers and alive with butterflies. "He used to use it as a retreat for his less admissible hobbies. That's why he had his bed installed on the ground floor. He said it was easier to get to when you were legless. Of course, beer wasn't his only 'hobby.' There were various easygoing ladies, and he could let them in and out discreetly through the French windows."

"What about your mother?"

"They were fond of each other, but they led their own lives. She didn't mind his friends, and he was discreet. I was only fourteen when she died, but I somehow knew the truth for a long time before that. What is it?" He'd seen a shadow come over her face.

She shook her head without answering and instead of pressing her he went on, "I'm afraid I was a disappointment to my father. His way of life shocked me a little. He thought I was very odd."

"That's what royal marriages are like, though, aren't they?"

"Some of them. It wouldn't have suited me."

"But," she knew it was risky to pursue this but she didn't seem able to stop, "if you had to marry someone you didn't really want to, it would be forgivable, wouldn't it?"

"No it wouldn't," he said, so forcefully that she jumped. "If you're hinting about lovers Dottie, let me warn you to forget it. I won't be a complaisant husband."

"Don't be silly," she said, coloring and trying to hide her pleasure. "Anyway, who says I was talking about me?"

"Didn't we agree to leave the baggage of the past behind? Don't do this Dottie, please." He laid his fingertips across her mouth. "There are some subjects we should never mention."

She longed to say, "What about Sophie?" but she couldn't get the words out in the face of his determination to silence her. And wasn't he right? If they could leave their awkward beginnings behind and start a new page, mightn't there be happiness that way?

Taking her hand, he led her deeper into the wood until they reached a place among the trees where the land sloped down then rose gently on the other side. The little valley was a mass of plants and small bushes, and on this side stood a small building made of heavy logs. He took her inside and Dottie looked around in delight.

"It's like a little cottage," she said.

"It's a 'hide' where you can watch animals and birds. My father had it built. Our happiest times together were spent here. And since he died I've sometimes come here alone. It's quiet and blessedly peaceful, and the noise of the world can't touch you." He indicated a rustic bed by the wall. "Sometimes I stay all night. The best time is in the dawn."

There was a large window where watchers could sit in the shadows, and Dottie went to sit by one, looking out ecstatically at the quiet scene. Now and then a soft rustle in the undergrowth revealed the presence of an animal. Sometimes she actually saw one. Or a bird hopped close, never knowing itself to be watched.

"Time for supper," Randolph murmured, close to her.

"It can't be, it's only...good heavens, we've been here hours."

"Yes, that's how it is. This place casts its spell and you forget everything else...almost everything else." He took her hand. "Come, let's go back to supper, and afterward, we will sit chastely holding hands."

"You dare and you're dead."

It was wonderful to hear his laughter echoing up into the branches, and see the flock of startled birds rise into the air.

The days passed in a haze of summer. Once it rained and they stayed indoors, leaving the French windows open, lying in bed, watching the shower. The nights merged into one night.

One morning she awoke in the early hours, and lay for a moment without opening her eyes. She was lying on her face and she could feel a slight chill on her back that told her the bedclothes had been removed. Fingertips were sliding softly across her skin, touching her so lightly that she could hardly feel them, but there was no doubt about the sensations they were creating. She gave a deep sigh of pleasurable content.

His fingers had reached her spine, moving down it in a leisurely, lingering fashion until they reached the small of her back. There they suddenly vanished, to be replaced by his lips, beginning the return journey. She shivered with delight and tried to turn over, but he prevented her.

"Keep still," he whispered. "I haven't finished yet."

"Just keep on as long as you like," she murmured blissfully. "At least...no, I don't mean that, because sooner or later I want you to do something else."

His lips were working on the back of her neck

while his hands traced her spine down and cupped her behind.

"I've wanted to do this," he said, "ever since the day I found you naked in the cupboard." She gave a deep throated chuckle that shivered through him, straight to his loins and made him take a sharp breath.

"I remember that day," she said. "You were so shocked."

"Shocked at myself. You were so lovely. I tried not to notice, but I couldn't manage it. And now, here you are, and you're all mine."

"Getting possessive, eh?"

"Any man, looking at you, would get possessive."

She rolled onto her back so fast that she took him by surprise. "Men aren't the only ones who get possessive," she said as her arms closed around him with a strength born of newly discovered passion. "Come here."

"My darling—"

"I said come here."

They had been married a week, just a few days, but long enough for her to change into a woman of fierce needs, determined to fulfill them. This was her lovemaking and with her words and her movements she let him know what she wanted. Having seized the initiative, she kept it. Randolph grinned, understanding perfectly, and not minding in the least when she said fiercely, "Now, *now!*"

Just as she'd learned about her own body she'd also learned about his and she put her knowledge to use, demanding the power and vigor of his loins for her exclusive pleasure.

"You're wrong," she whispered mischievously. "It's you who are all *mine.*"

"Your Majesty's obedient servant," he said, falling in with her mood.

"So I should hope. Oh Randolph. *Randolph...*"

Later, remembering that enchanted time, Dottie found that it wasn't only the passion that stayed in her mind.

For one thing, there was the dog.

He appeared one day in front of the hide where they were watching together, and turned a hopeful face on them. He was a tramp among dogs, scruffy, muddy and with no one part of him matching any other. Dottie was immediately won over by his goofy charm, but she could imagine Randolph's reaction to this disgraceful creature.

Then she heard a soft whistle and looked up to see him grinning. He whistled again and opened the door of the hide. There were still scraps from their meal on the table, and he proceeded to offer these to the visitor, who wolfed them down. Seeing her regarding him with raised eyebrows, Randolph colored and said self-consciously, "I had a dog like this when I was a child."

"You? Like this?"

"Yes, he was a stray that I adopted, but only for five minutes. My mother didn't like dogs, said they were messy creatures, and made me get rid of it."

"What did your father say?" Dottie demanded indignantly.

"Nothing. He never interfered in domestic matters. That was her price for turning a blind eye to the way he lived. He sent him to the stables where he probably had a happier life than he would have done in a palace."

"Perhaps it was because it was a mongrel. Maybe a pedigree dog would have been better."

"She disliked all dogs. But I wanted a mongrel. Everything around me was pedigreed. My friends were chosen for me from among the aristocracy. Some of them I liked well enough, but it's not the same as choosing for yourself. And 'royalty must keep a proper distance,' even from friends."

"That's terrible," Dottie said, aghast. "No wonder you're so...so..."

"Yes, no wonder," he said, understanding what she couldn't say. "Fritz, my dog, was everything the others weren't. He came from the wrong side of the tracks. He didn't have a bloodline—not a respectable one, anyway. He was spontaneous and he didn't understand rules. I can't tell you how attractive that was to a boy who was just beginning to understand how rules had to govern his life, and there was no escape for him."

The light was fading fast but Dottie didn't light the lamp they sometimes used. She had a feeling that the darkness was helping him. This was a man who didn't confide his feelings easily, but today something had made it happen.

"What a pity that your mother couldn't ease up," she said slowly, "just to make you happy."

"She loved me in her way, but to her everything was subordinate to being royal. When I was old enough I had to give her a formal bow when we met in the morning. She was the queen, and only after that was she my mother. It wasn't her fault, it was the way she was raised."

"Poor little boy!" Dottie murmured.

"It's sweet of you to say so, but don't feel sorry for me. That little boy doesn't exist anymore."

He was so wrong, she thought. That lonely little boy was here with them this minute, so real that she felt she knew him. Such love as he'd received had come from a mother too rigid to show him real affection. His father had been kindly but weak, too selfish to limit his own pleasures to stand up for his son. Had anybody in Randolph's whole life loved him warmly, tenderly, unconditionally?

Yes.

She couldn't say, "It's all right, you've got me now," because that would be to venture onto his private ground where he was still uneasy of intruders. He'd allowed her in, just a little, but there was a long way to go yet. But she could be patient.

The dog was gulping the last of the tidbits noisily.

"I expect he'll stay with you now," she observed.

But the next moment a cry of "Brin!" came through the trees. The dog grabbed one last morsel of food, leapt onto the table and vanished through the window. From the distance came cries of welcome from childish voices.

"Obviously that was Brin," Randolph said wryly.

Dottie took his hand and squeezed it. "Never mind. *I* come from the wrong side of the tracks. Will I do?"

He slipped his arm around her, and spoke more tenderly than she had ever heard. "I think you'll do very well, my Dottie."

That night, for the first time, he slept with his head on her breast, and her arms around him.

The next day Dottie found a man who bred German shepherds and arranged to have a litter of three brought to Kellensee for Randolph's inspection. He chose one, but Dottie fell in love with the others and they ended up keeping them all. A visit to a local animal sanctuary produced two cats, but after that Randolph begged her to stop.

Then there was the time Bertha discovered a pair of paparazzi and managed to send them both flying into the duck pond. Grinning, Randolph complimented her, but added that her technique wasn't a patch on Dottie's.

The newspapers arrived and piled up, unnoticed. When she could spare time to read about their own wedding Dottie found herself studying a picture of the moment she'd tossed her bouquet. She was looking away from Randolph, into the crowd, but he was watching her with an expression that made her catch her breath.

The headline called it The Look Of Love. Underneath it the caption said, *Those who thought this was nothing but a state marriage had their answer today in the look of adoration the groom turned on his bride.*

Dottie studied Randolph's face longingly. Adoration? It could be read that way. He was smiling, oblivious of everything but his bride, the very picture of a man entering on his greatest joy.

But why did he never let her see that look?

She heard footsteps and hastily thrust the newspaper under a cushion, going quickly out to meet Randolph and be told that a deer had been seen near the hide, and they should hurry.

By day their happiest times were spent in the hide. Birds and animals came and went while they watched, entranced, in silence. In those silences she felt herself growing closer to him. She'd thought so often of what they might say, but now she knew that words were unnecessary. He'd brought her to the place nearest his heart, and allowed her in, and that counted, even though she'd had to nudge him.

"Why were you reluctant to bring me here?" she asked once as they sat by the window in the fading light.

"That isn't true, Dottie."

"You never suggested it until I turned down Rome and New York."

"I thought you'd find them more exciting. Don't you want to see the world?"

She smiled. "Do you have a world better than this?"

"No." He smiled back. "There isn't one."

"We will come back, won't we? Often."

"That will be for Your Majesty to say," he teased.

"No it won't. You're officially Prince Consort now. And about that, you never said anything."

"I said thank you. It was our wedding day. Did you expect me to think about anything but you?" His voice became teasing. "I was a little disturbed to find my wife's mind fixed on state affairs while she was dancing with *me.* Seriously, I do thank you. It's just that such things seem less important now."

"Wait until we get home and a mountain of paperwork descends on you. I give it all back. Well, most of it. You'll run the country much better than I could."

"Dottie," he said, shocked. "Surely not because I'm a man? Don't disillusion me."

"No, you idiot," she said, laughing. "Because you've had years of training, and you know all the things about this country that I don't. I'm going back to school. I need to know Elluria's history, which means,'' she gave a gloomy sigh, ''I need to know every other country's history, too.''

''Cobblers!'' Randolph said sympathetically.

''Right. Oh heck, what have I let myself in for? There's so much for me to learn, and while I'm doing that someone must keep things going. I've managed so far on a smile and a load of chutzpah, but it's not enough for the years ahead.''

''What a wise woman you are,'' he said tenderly.

''But don't think you're going to have it all your own way.''

''That thought never crossed my mind,'' he said truthfully.

''I still want my parliamentary reforms in time for the next election and I'll be breathing down your neck to make sure I get them.''

''Just like before, really.''

''But you can do as you like with the boring stuff.''

''Thank you, Dottie. Your faith in me is deeply moving.''

''You don't fool me.''

''And *you* don't fool *me*. This is nothing but a trick to off-load 'the boring stuff' onto me, leaving you free to indulge in a good fight whenever the mood takes you. Oh no! We'll be a team. It works better that way. To be honest, I was never much good at the smile and the chutzpah.''

''You're getting better at them.''

''Only when you're around. But you're not getting off that easily. Stick to your studies. I hear your languages are coming on splendidly. Your tutor says you have a natural ear. Your German is excellent, your French not far behind.'' A sense of mischief that he'd never known he possessed made him add, "One day you may even stop mangling the English language."

She gave him a gentle thump. "I'll get you for that, just you wait!"

He murmured softly in her ear, "Must I wait?"

His breath tickled her ear and sent scurryings of pleasure through her. "Randolph, I'm trying to be serious."

"So am I. Very serious." His lips were at work on the soft skin of her neck, distracting her.

"It's important."

He rose, drawing her with him, and moving toward the bed. "What could be more important than this?"

"But we were discussing urgent matters of state."

"*Hang* urgent matters of state."

Chapter Twelve

As the summer faded people looked anxiously at the sky and feared for the weather on coronation day. But the morning dawned pale and clear, with no clouds in the sky, and the promise of warmth to come. As she was picking at tea and toast, having no appetite for more, Dottie took a phone call from her head groom.

"With Your Majesty's permission I believe we could risk the open carriage."

"I agree," she said with relief.

As her ladies dressed her Aunt Liz remarked, "People would have been so disappointed not to see you properly."

"Yes, it's really their day," Dottie agreed, turning a little to survey the coronation gown in the long mirror. It was a magnificent creation in cream satin, embroidered with the four emblems of Elluria, each one studded with tiny diamonds. More diamonds were worked into the curve of the neckline, and in the long train that stretched behind her.

"What a day!" Aunt Liz enthused. "Who would have thought it would ever happen?"

"Nobody," Dottie murmured, "because it shouldn't have."

How could she tell anyone that her heart was heavy on what should have been her day of triumph? Who would ever understand that she was miserable at what today would do to the man she loved? This should have been Randolph's coronation. Instead he would hand her to the place that should have been his, and swear loyalty to her with her other subjects. And he would do it with a smile on his face.

That smile scared her, because he never told her of the pain that lay beneath it. It was kind, tender, understanding, and it shut her out. But surely, today of all days, he would give her a glimpse of his true feelings?

"Leave me for a moment," she said suddenly.

Her ladies, who had been fussing about her, curtsied and withdrew. Dottie paced the floor, feeling a dozen years older than the unaware girl who'd arrived here six months ago. She stopped at the open French windows, looking out onto the park, where the colors of autumn were just being seen. This was the day when her future should stretch ahead, clear and triumphant. Instead it was shrouded in mist.

She turned at the sound of the door. It was Randolph, and she thought he had never looked more splendid.

"Are you quite ready?" he asked.

"I shall never be ready for this," she burst out. "It's all wrong. This should be your day."

"It is the day we shall share," he told her gravely.

"No, no," she shook her head. "That's just pretty words. I'm stealing what should be yours and I don't know how not to. I'm not really queen and we both know it."

"Listen to me," he said, shushing her as he took her hands between his. "I told you once before that you must believe in yourself before anybody else can do so. That was never more true than now. You have made the throne your own, not through your ancestors, but with your heart. You've won your people's love, and because of that they are truly your people."

"But I was given the chance. You'd have taken it, too."

He shook his head. "No, I never knew how. They respected me, but they didn't love me. I've always done my duty, and thought that was enough. It was you who showed me that duty could—should—be done joyfully, so that people's hearts reached out to you. I never had the gift of winning hearts."

"You won mine."

"Yes, and that's my best hope. When they see that you love me, they may think I'm not so bad after all."

She couldn't bear that. To the horror of both of them she burst into tears.

"Dottie, Dottie..." he drew her close. "Don't cry."

She couldn't stop. The sadness of his resignation overwhelmed her. She'd never wept for herself, but she wept bitterly for him.

"That's enough," Randolph urged her, half tender,

half commanding. And when she still couldn't stop he gave her a little shake. "Listen Dottie, for I'm speaking very seriously now. This is the twenty-first century. Kings and queens have survived a long time, but we can't go on in the old way, depending on respect, fear or power. Now our people have to want us. They have to love us. And it's you that they love. It's you that has the power to take this monarchy, this country, into the future. I know it, and your people know it. So now go out to them, and let them see that you are theirs. This is your day of glory."

"But it should have been yours," she said huskily as he dried her eyes.

"Is there only one kind of glory then? Haven't we discovered another kind?"

He spoke softly in the voice he used at night when there was only the darkness and their passion, but Dottie couldn't let herself off the hook that easily.

"Yes, we have, but you know you need more than that. You know you couldn't be happy if you weren't doing your job."

"But I shall be doing it, through you. It's the same. Hush…" he laid a finger over her lips. "There are things about me you don't know yet. They can only be told at the right time, and perhaps that time will never come. Try to trust me, and believe this, that there is no bitterness in my heart today. Only love for you. My darling, why can't you believe me?"

"Because… Oh, I can't wrap it up in posh words."

He laughed. "That's my Dottie. Blunt to the end. Be blunt then, and tell me why you can't believe that I love you."

"Because it's your duty to love me. And you always do your duty."

"Is that what you think? Only duty and no more? Dottie, Dottie what a short memory you have. Haven't there been nights when I've held you against my heart and we've been soul of each other's soul as well as flesh of each other's flesh?"

"Yes," she said wistfully. "I've felt that then, but why have you never actually said you loved me before?"

"Because I didn't want to win your contempt. Don't you remember once saying to me, 'Would you have been crass enough to try to make me think you were in love with me? I suppose I should be grateful to have been spared that piece of dishonesty.'? My darling, blinkered Dottie, how was I supposed to speak of love after that?"

"But I...I didn't mean it. I was angry. I'd have said anything."

"That I believe," he said with a touch of humor. "But when you stopped being angry, you didn't take it back."

"How could I?"

"Hush. We tangled ourselves in such a web, and words only made it worse. I tried to show you my love and hoped you'd understand, but you seemed to be pining for Mike..."

"Not really. I've loved you longer than you think. It was Sophie I was afraid of."

"Never fear, and never doubt." He drew her close and laid his lips on hers, caressing them tenderly. "Do you doubt me now...and now?"

If only they would all go away, she thought, and leave the two of them alone in the place where they could love and be happy. But the world couldn't be shut out for long. A noise in the outer room made them sigh and draw apart.

"There will be later for us," Randolph said. "Now you belong to your people."

"Not without you," she said urgently.

"I am always beside you."

She stood for a moment, composing herself. Meeting Randolph's eyes, she saw his slight gesture indicating that she should lift her chin, and did so. His smile reassured her.

Her ladies were waiting to attach the heavy ermine and velvet cloak to her shoulders. She took Randolph's arm and they walked out of the state apartments into the broad corridor. To left and right of them people were curtseying and she smiled. This was her day, because Randolph had given it to her. Now she would take what he had given, and make of it something better still.

Down the grand stairway, left along the crimson carpet to where the sun gleamed in the courtyard, then out through the wide arch to the open carriage. The waiting crowds cheered as they appeared and at first she acknowledged them, but the next moment, Dottie-like, she forgot regal dignity in the excitement of a discovery.

"It's him," she told Randolph. "It's Jack, leading the horses."

Before he could speak she slipped away to where the head groom stood holding Jack's bridle. The old horse stood proud and beautiful, a plume nodding from his head.

"It'll be his last outing, ma'am," the coachman

said proudly. "But I promised him he wouldn't miss this great day."

"I'm so glad." She planted a swift kiss on Jack's forehead. "It wouldn't have been the same without him."

"Dottie," Randolph said patiently, "I'm glad to see him too, but can we get on with the coronation?"

Smiling she took his hand and let him hand her into the carriage. The crowd, who'd understood what was happening, cheered louder than ever. That was Dottie, their queen.

The carriage door slammed behind them, then a signal to the horses and they were on the move out of the palace gates. Bunting flew in the breeze overhead, more bunting was draped from the lamp posts, almost everyone in the crowd seemed to be waving a little flag.

As they drew up outside the cathedral Randolph turned to her. "Remember," he said. "Together."

"Together."

The cathedral was cool and dark as they entered it. There was the master of ceremonies watching their arrival, clutching a mobile phone with which to alert the organist. It all went smoothly and at the exact moment that they stepped forward the organ pealed out overhead.

Dottie had expected this part to be a blur. Instead she found her senses heightened so that she could hear each note of the music and pick out individual faces. Almost every country had sent a representative to her coronation.

Near the front she saw Prince Harold and his princess, invited because diplomacy demanded it. Sophie's face was a mask, but Harold was watching the procession near, and something told Dottie that he was tensed as a coiled spring. She could almost feel the waves of anger radiating from him.

She and Randolph slowed to a halt in front of the archbishop, solemn and splendid in his golden vestments. The organ faded to silence and the archbishop raised his voice to declare, "This is a glorious day—"

"It's a day of dishonor!"

The shout died away, leaving behind a stunned silence. Into that silence Harold's voice came again.

"This is a day of dishonor, the day Elluria crowns an impostor with no right to the throne." He stepped out into the aisle and advanced on Dottie and Randolph who'd turned to face him.

"Be silent," Randolph commanded him.

"You expect me to be silent while I'm cheated of my rights?" Harold screamed. "It's a conspiracy. This woman is not the true heir."

He snatched a paper from an inner pocket and turned to face the startled congregation, waving it aloft. "She is not the true heir," he shouted again. "She springs from a bastard line, and here is the proof."

"Nonsense!" Durmand bustled forward, angry and businesslike. "This has all been dealt with. Her Majesty's line has been checked back to Duke Egbert and found to be direct."

"Direct but not legitimate," Harold sneered. "Egbert never had a child by his lawful wife. His daughter was the product of an extramarital liaison with a housemaid."

"But that is nonsense," Durmand protested. "He could never have passed her off as his wife's child."

"He could in those days," Harold snapped. "And with his wife's connivance. Don't forget what a long time it took Egbert and his wife to travel from Elluria to England. A journey of a few days took months, and why?"

"Because they lingered to enjoy themselves," Durmand said helplessly.

"Because it was easier to perpetuate a fraud in another country," Harold shouted. "The child was born in Switzerland, where nobody had ever seen either woman. They stayed in an out-of-the-way house in the country, the maid gave birth, the doctor was told he was attending the duchess. How was he to know otherwise?"

"But the duchess would never have agreed—" Durmand protested.

"Why not? People had jeered at her as too old to give her husband a child. After that the jeers stopped, and she traveled on to England with 'her' baby in her arms. The maid was bought off and thrown out. But she talked and the story has been preserved."

Enderlin stepped in, as much Dottie's champion as he had been her combatant. "But nobody heard of it until now," he said. "It's surfaced too conveniently for my liking."

"And might never have surfaced at all," Sophie said, speaking for the first time. "But for the invaluable assistant of Mr. Michael Kenton."

"Mike?" Dottie exclaimed. "I don't believe it."

"We had such an interesting talk the night of the ball," Sophie continued, turning directly to Dottie. "He repeated tales he'd heard from your grandfather, when he was in his cups, and there was enough to put us on the trail."

"But that was ages ago," Dottie exclaimed. "Why wait until now?"

"It was just a rumor," Harold said. "It's taken until now to get the proof, hidden in the Swiss archives." He waved his papers again. "But the proof is here. Examine it. In the meantime I demand that this false coronation is called off."

Through the whirling of Dottie's head only one thing was clear. If Harold was clever enough to make this credible, Randolph would lose everything for the second time. She herself would lose the friends she'd made and the country she'd come to love, but it was for him that her heart ached.

"Randolph," she said, clasping his hand.

"It's all right, my darling. Everything is going to be all right."

"But can this be true?"

"It wouldn't surprise me at all," he said calmly. "Old Egbert was very free with his attentions. I should think he had any number of liaisons. He undoubtedly married his wife for her money and she was some years older than him. It all sounds very likely. How fortunate that it didn't come to light before."

"But, Randolph...what difference does that make? It's out now, and that means I can't be the queen and—"

"It means no such thing. Trust me Dottie, I'll make you a queen before the day's out."

Sophie was regarding Dottie with a mixture of triumph and malevolence. Harold and Durmand were having a shouting match, with Harold's voice growing shriller every moment.

"This woman is an impostor. She should be arrested for offenses against the state."

"But you'll never get the king to agree to that," Randolph observed mildly.

Harold rounded on him. "I am the king."

"No," Randolph said, still in the same mild tone. "*I* am." Ignoring Harold's sneer he went on, "I have been king of Elluria since the moment of my father's death."

If Harold's announcement produced consternation this one caused turmoil. Everyone was staring at Randolph as if unable to believe their ears, but his glance was for Dottie, as though only her reaction mattered to him.

"Your researchers have been hard at work, Harold, but so have mine. And I too have found something interesting. It concerns Ellie Trentworth, the young woman with whom my father went through a form of marriage. I say 'a form of marriage' because it wasn't worth the paper it was written on. Ellie already had a husband, two in fact. Probably more than two. Goodness knows who she was really married to, but it certainly wasn't my father.

"So the 'form of marriage' had no basis in law. It was invalid, leaving him as much a bachelor afterward as before, and therefore free to marry my mother. There never was a stain on their marriage, or my legitimacy."

Harold had gone very pale but he recovered himself.

"Words," he scoffed. "Where is your proof?"

"Here," Randolph said, pulling some papers from inside his jacket. "These are the marriage certificates of Ellie Trentworth to both husbands. Since I discovered the truth I've kept them on me at all times. I had a feeling I might need to produce them at a moment's notice, especially today.''

Harold snatched at the papers. The whole cathedral seemed to be holding its breath as he went through them.

''These are forgeries,'' he snapped. ''I don't believe any of it.''

But Sophie believed it. As she saw her last chance vanish she screamed and went into hysterics. Nothing else could have so effectively demolished Harold's claim, and two soldiers moved discreetly to take their places behind him. Sophie's sobs grew louder, prompting him to hiss, ''Shut up!''

''This is most irregular,'' the archbishop said worriedly, looking at Dottie. ''Is this lady of legitimate descent, or isn't she?''

''It doesn't matter, since she makes no claim to the throne,'' Randolph said. ''Indeed, she never did make a claim to the throne. It was forced on her, and she accepted it as a duty, and from love. But it was based on a misapprehension. The mistaken belief that I was illegitimate because my parents' marriage was bigamous. These certificates prove otherwise.''

Durmand was studying the papers with increasing delight. ''Then the marriage was valid, and your claim to the throne cannot be challenged,'' he told Randolph. ''You are, and have always been, the rightful king.''

''You need never have brought me here at all,'' Dottie breathed. ''Randolph, how long have you known about this?''

''I discovered soon after you arrived in Elluria.''

Her brain whirled. ''You mean...before we married?''

"Yes."

She couldn't speak. The implications were so enormous, so wonderful, that she didn't dare believe them. "But why did you keep quiet?" she asked at last. "If you'd spoken then you wouldn't have needed to marry me."

He put his hands on either side of her face and spoke in a voice deep with tenderness. "Darling, beloved Dottie, I wanted to marry you. I *longed* to marry you. I've loved you since the day we met in London, when you took me out of the narrow, constricted world I'd known, and showed me another world that could be mine, but only if you were there. Since then I've plotted and schemed, pulled strings, behaved unethically, broken rules, all to keep you with me. You made the sun shine for me, and I knew if I lost you the sun would never shine again.

"I was afraid that if you learned the truth, you'd pack your bags and go. I couldn't face the thought of losing the only woman I have ever loved. It was a deception, but one for which you will, perhaps, forgive me?"

"But you could have been king all this time," she breathed, still not daring to be convinced by the love she saw in his eyes, a love that more than matched her own.

"Earlier today I told you that there were things you don't know about me, and perhaps never would, because they could only be told at the right time. Now that time has come." He raised his voice. "I call on everyone here to witness that I would rather be your consort than king, and married to any other woman."

The congregation broke into loud applause. The royal guests in the front row rose to their feet and were followed by row after row behind them, clapping and cheering. High up aloft the choirboys joined in.

But Randolph and Dottie saw only each other. His gaze said that this was the measure of how much she mattered to him. She was more to him than his duty, more than his life. She *was* his life. She was awed by the sacrifice he'd been prepared to make, rather than lose her.

The archbishop's worried voice broke in on them. "But can we have a coronation or not?"

"Of course we can," Dottie told him. "The coronation of Elluria's rightful monarch, King Randolph."

"And his consort, Queen Dorothea," Randolph put in, "who reigns as supremely in her subjects' hearts and she does in her husband's."

Taking her hand in his he stepped forward and they stood side by side as the archbishop raised his voice, calling to the people.

"I present to you, Randolph, your sovereign lord, rightful king of Elluria, and his lady..."

She barely heard the rest. The mist that had shrouded the path ahead had lifted now, and she could see clearly at last. This was the world they would share; years of work and duty, made sweet to each by the presence of the other. Behind them stretched the way back out of the cathedral, and beyond that lay the sunshine.

* * * * *

Where royalty and romance go hand in hand...

The series continues in Silhouette Romance with these unforgettable novels:

HER ROYAL HUSBAND
by Cara Colter
on sale July 2002 (SR #1600)

THE PRINCESS HAS AMNESIA!
by Patricia Thayer
on sale August 2002 (SR #1606)

SEARCHING FOR HER PRINCE
by Karen Rose Smith
on sale September 2002 (SR #1612)

And look for more Crown and Glory stories in SILHOUETTE DESIRE starting in October 2002!

Available at your favorite retail outlet.

Visit Silhouette at www.eHarlequin.com

SRCAG

If you enjoyed what you just read, then we've got an offer you can't resist!

Take 2 bestselling love stories FREE!

Plus get a FREE surprise gift!

Clip this page and mail it to Silhouette Reader Service™

IN U.S.A.
3010 Walden Ave.
P.O. Box 1867
Buffalo, N.Y. 14240-1867

IN CANADA
P.O. Box 609
Fort Erie, Ontario
L2A 5X3

YES! Please send me 2 free Silhouette Special Edition® novels and my free surprise gift. After receiving them, if I don't wish to receive anymore, I can return the shipping statement marked cancel. If I don't cancel, I will receive 6 brand-new novels every month, before they're available in stores! In the U.S.A., bill me at the bargain price of $3.99 plus 25¢ shipping and handling per book and applicable sales tax, if any*. In Canada, bill me at the bargain price of $4.74 plus 25¢ shipping and handling per book and applicable taxes**. That's the complete price and a savings of at least 10% off the cover prices—what a great deal! I understand that accepting the 2 free books and gift places me under no obligation ever to buy any books. I can always return a shipment and cancel at any time. Even if I never buy another book from Silhouette, the 2 free books and gift are mine to keep forever.

235 SDN DNUR
335 SDN DNUS

Name (PLEASE PRINT)

Address Apt.#

City State/Prov. Zip/Postal Code

* Terms and prices subject to change without notice. Sales tax applicable in N.Y.
** Canadian residents will be charged applicable provincial taxes and GST.
All orders subject to approval. Offer limited to one per household and not valid to current Silhouette Special Edition® subscribers.
® are registered trademarks of Harlequin Books S.A., used under license.

SPED02 ©1998 Harlequin Enterprises Limited

buy books

Your one-stop shop for great reads at great prices. We have all your favorite Harlequin, Silhouette, MIRA and Steeple Hill books, as well as a host of other bestsellers in Other Romances. Discover a wide array of new releases, bargains and hard-to-find books today!

learn to write

Become the writer you always knew you could be: get tips and tools on how to craft the perfect romance novel and have your work critiqued by professional experts in romance fiction. Follow your dream now!

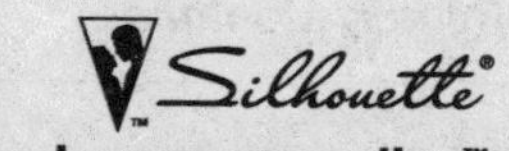

Where love comes alive™—online...

Visit us at
www.eHarlequin.com

SINTLTW

MONTANA MAVERICKS

One of Silhouette Special Edition's most popular series returns with three sensational stories filled with love, small-town gossip, reunited lovers, a little murder, hot nights and the best in romance:

HER MONTANA MAN
by Laurie Paige
(ISBN#: 0-373-24483-5)
Available August 2002

BIG SKY COWBOY
by Jennifer Mikels
(ISBN#: 0-373-24491-6)
Available September 2002

MONTANA LAWMAN
by Allison Leigh
(ISBN#: 0-373-24497-5)
Available October 2002

True love is the only way to beat the heat in Rumor, Montana....

Visit Silhouette at www.eHarlequin.com SSEMON02